THE WALKING

BY THE SAME AUTHOR

The Age of Orphans

The Walking

Laleh Khadivi

BLOOMSBURY CIRCUS
LONDON • NEW DELHI • NEW YORK • SYDNEY

First published in Great Britain 2013

Bloomsbury Circus is an imprint of Bloomsbury Publishing Plc
50 Bedford Square, London WC1B 3DP

www.bloomsbury.com
www.bloomsburycircus.com

Bloomsbury Publishing, London, New Delhi, New York and Sydney

A CIP catalogue record for this book is available from the British Library

ISBN 978 1 4088 1484 0
10 9 8 7 6 5 4 3 2 1

Typeset by Hewer Text UK Ltd, Edinburgh
Printed and bound in Great Britain by CPI Group (UK) Ltd, Croydon CR0 4YY

To those with the courage to leave,
and to those with the courage to stay.

All vertebrates . . . spend time learning their surroundings and for the most part migrate within these familiar areas. On the other hand, all plants and all other invertebrates . . . are always traveling on into the unknown, through not, as one might suppose, randomly or haphazardly.

—Dr. Robin Baker
The Mystery of Migration

I know not how significant it is, or how far it is an evidence of singularity, that an individual should thus consent in his pettiest walk with the general movement of the race; but I know that something akin to the migratory instinct of birds and quadrupeds . . . affects both nations and individuals, either perennially or from time to time.

—Henry David Thoreau
Walking

Why should we plant the tree we will never see?

—Abolqasem Ferdowsi
Shahnameh

FLIGHT

EVERYWHERE, WE ARE leaving.

In desert villages, mountain towns and old cities, the worried minds hum with decision-making, decisions made. We meet in groups to talk it over, to look into the eyes of family, lovers and dear friends and ask.

Do we go?

Hands reach out, cigarettes are smoked, cup after cup of tea is taken and the talk is talked until the time comes and radios are turned on, turned up, and we are silent at the sounds of the afternoon news.

Today the venerable Ayatollah Ruholla Khomeini took his place as supreme leader . . . today the exiled Shah was denied asylum in France . . . today two million took to Azadi Square in Tehran to voice their independence from the manipulative forces of the British, the Americans . . .

Radios are turned down, turned off, but the news stays. It hangs heavy in the air of rooms where we gather to watch night fall and ask the questions that come, urgent without pause.

Where then?

For how long?

What to take? What to leave?

Hands rummage in pockets, over prayer beads, into knitting, cooking and games, to any thoughtless actions that free our minds to work furiously on this new knot that jumbles the threads of our lives.

Yes, now the Shah is gone and that is good, but who knows what the mullahs want for us?

We have suffocated under the Shah and now we will suffocate under this regime of Allah and Allah and Allah.

We audition hopeful outcomes.

This is the worst of it. The people will settle.

It cannot stay like this forever.

Don't worry. Everything will fall back into place. It always does.

And for the night, nothing is decided, and through sleep and into dreams, questions are asked, talk is talked, this side and that.

We must go.

Must we?

Yes. For our dignity. For our future. For a chance. This new regime is not capable of dignity. I heard just the other day, Mehri Khanoum was walking down the streets and they approached her, told her to wipe the vanity off her lips, a razor blade hidden in the napkin . . . just like that.

I heard, the mass hangings . . .

I heard a stoning in the square . . .

Other voices said, Sit for a minute, have a chai, let us think it through.

You know, this is Iran, regimes are like seasons, always passing, always changing.

I say it is a good thing this corrupt Shah is gone. Let us just wait. Just watch.

Ack! This mullah will go too, give him a few years and some other scourge will take his place. Who knows what tomorrow holds? Not I. We know what only God knows? Relax. Here, there, go, stay, problems are everywhere. At least here I am a man among my countrymen. You are a woman among your sisters, and outside our window is a world where we see our faces in the faces we see. Show me another world like that and I might follow you there.

Even so, many are gone before the New Year.

If yes, we go the way all the natural world goes, first a few and then the flood. And new decisions must be made.

I will go alone. No, it's best, let us go, he and I, and then we will send for you. Give me a few weeks to settle in, an apartment, jobs, visas. What if we sent the children ahead? They will be safe in school. It is complicated, but safer. It is simple, but more dangerous.

And decisions after those.

Do we go by foot? By bus? Which border is still open? There is a smuggler, to the south, for a price . . . we have some money. We have enough money to go by plane. By plane while we still can. It is fastest, the most certain.

And the decisions after that.

Leave it all. Take it all. Bring only one suitcase. Bring the suitcase and the old photos. Bring nothing but the two rugs from Tabriz.

Yes, Baba's rugs. No, not to sell. Just to have. We must have that, have something, at least.

Like that we are gone.

We cannot decide how we arrive, but in the end, we are all received the same. Those of us who wheel our belongings out of customs into a hive of waiting relatives at LAX are no different from those of us with scraped palms and bruised kneecaps who linger in cheap rooms in Frankfurt, Milan or Karachi waiting for the next piece of luck or we who stand in long embassy lines until it is our turn to announce.

I am Baha'i. They have burned my home for my beliefs.

I am Jewish. Our father and uncles have been missing for two months.

I am Kurdish. My blood alone is a death sentence in this new regime.

And we—the welcomed, the waiting, the persecuted—are not that different from the dreamer who follows a trail of wanderlust that leads him to America, where he arrives excited and alone, ready to be taken by that which does not welcome or reject any of us: the streets, the sidewalk, the California sea.

A SEND-OFF

AS SALADIN PLANNED his sendoff, a party.

In his mind he invites them all. His brother, Ali; his four sisters; his father, who will not come, so deep does the abandonment cut into his pride. A few friends from school. Mr. Hosseini the English teacher and Ahmed the projectionist and of course Haleh, which means of course her sister, which means he will have to divide his attentions between the two or recruit Ali to share the duty of entertaining the prettiest sisters in the mountain town. Either way, Haleh will wear her famous purple mini-jupe, stand beside the table of sweets and let her eyes well with tears that Saladin brushes from her cheeks with his thumb as he whispers, *It is only for a year, or two. Then you will join me, you must.* A feast of favorite dishes—gorhmeh sabzi, joojeh kebab, shirin pollo—all prepared without his request, without even his want, and laid out on the sofre like the last of all food. And music, all night there is music. Pepino, Adamo, the Beatles, and in case anyone should mistake his destination, a lot of Elvis and even more Beach Boys. Music and much dancing in the pressed shirt and creased jeans and sunglasses that don't come off until the evening's end when everyone insists they must look into his eyes to more properly offer advice, well-wishes, envy and embraces. Saladin promises to write, to call, to come back as soon as he is rich, as soon as he is married, as soon as he can, but secretly hopes to shake all of it—the party, the sisters, the promises—off the instant his chest fills with the lightness of flight as the plane eases itself off the only earth he has ever known.

He plans for the joy of a departure inevitable, celebrated, long foreseen.

As it happened, their father woke them with angry shouts.

Posho! Saladin! Ali! Up!

The brothers knew better than to ask. They dressed randomly in the dark and climbed into the cab of the old military truck their father drove to work. A steady rain fell over them, but by the time the truck engine came to life, the wetness had evaporated off their arms and faces, leaving behind a slight damp in the places their bodies had touched. As they drove, the sky grew bright slowly, one degree for each cigarette their father lit, another degree every time he muttered. Say nothing. Follow their orders. Obey what they ask of you, what I ask. Then it will be done and they will leave us alone. God willing, they will leave us alone. God willing. Say nothing . . . like this he rambled until sunlight filled the slits between the clouds and made the rain shine silver. Only then did the old man go quiet.

Saladin closed his eyes and pressed his head against the window and tried to find the last of sleep. Why not? He had lived this all before. This early morning was the same as last early morning and the mornings before that. They would go to the barracks, where there would be some tension about an escaped Kurd farmer who had gone to Turkey or started a rebel faction in the mountains. They would go to his plot of land, wake his wife, demand to know where the guns or men were hiding, and after an hour of shouts and accusations and threats of violence, his father would lose steam and step off to some shade to smoke a cigarette and let Ali tidy what blankets and feed bowls and shoe piles had been upset in the lazy raid. If the wife was a fierce woman, as was common in the mountains, she followed them around and cursed the captain, called him a traitorous Kurd in humiliating service to the Shah. If she was exceptionally upset or exceptionally brave, she spat each time she said his name. Saladin waited in the cab of the truck, doors closed and windows rolled up, and watched it all like a movie with faint sound. Either way they always made it back to the barracks for the midday meal, followed by the idle afternoons that Saladin spent pestering the new cadet from Tehran with incessant questions. Are the cinemas bigger? How much bigger? Are they louder? How loud? And Ali presented their father with long, respectful arguments about the Kurdish cause and the Shah's most recent harassments and politely questioned the old man's confusing loyalties. But, Baba, Ali would always ask, if you are a Kurd, why do you police the Kurds? How come you answer to the Shah? Why does the Shah hate us so? Their father rarely answered, and if he did, it was brief. One day you will understand, Ali jaan. One day all of this will become clear. And then he would light a cigarette and fill the afternoon with a long classical poem that quieted the barracks and stopped the old janitor in the middle of his slow chores. Yes. Yes, Agha Captain. That is how I remember it. You sing it just like your father sang it, God save his soul.

On the morning they woke to shouts, nothing happened as it had happened before and Saladin woke from his half sleep against the truck window to find the streets in front of the barracks crowded with new trucks and jeeps and revolutionary guards, bearded men no older than Ali and somehow even more serious. They followed their father inside and no one stopped to salute him, to bid him good morning or to take his hat. All available bodies were occupied in the ordered busyness required to take apart the barracks and dismantle the hanging guns and ammunition and flags that had forever decorated the walls. The large painting of the king had been taken down and slashed three times, in perfect diagonal cuts that matched the direction of his many-colored sashes. Saladin walked to the painting. Up close the man was as ugly as he had been from afar. His eyes were snake set, and the artist could not pull any nobility from the shape of his head. Saladin remembered the day the portrait arrived, its first hanging on the high hook, the fanfare and courteous applause from the men who gathered nervously around their new police captain and his two young, light-eyed sons.

At their father's desk a mullah sat reading. When the family stood before him, he did not look up from his work, and when he did, he caught Saladin's eye. His voice was a disinterested whisper.

Do you think we have done a good job with the painting?

Saladin faced the mullah and said nothing. He was of middle age with a round head and a beard that seemed to stretch down from beneath his eyeballs all the way to the bottom of his neck. He wore his tall, gray turban wrapped tightly around his forehead, not loose and high at the hairline as was the Kurdish fashion. As he stood to walk toward them, great quantities of cleaned and ironed black fabric folded and unfolded around his legs. He took their father's hand and kissed him once on each cheek.

Khoshamadeem. It will be helpful for us to know that you and your family stand behind the Ayatollah.

His voice was fresh and certain and he kept the old man's hand pressed between his.

Their father looked down and spoke to the floor.

Of course.

The mullah dropped their father's hand.

Of course what, Captain? Be specific. These are not casual times.

Of course my sons and I know the time of the Shah is over. Of course. Everyone must know.

To hear obedience from a mouth that had only ever given orders! Saladin looked away from it, from his father and the mullah and the old, familiar room that was beginning to lose solidity and shape. He focused on his feet, where by accident he had put on the Italian shoes he was saving for America. He cursed himself, the work he'd have to do to clean and polish them, and stared at the shined black boots of the revolutionary guards as they stepped over the edges and ends of furniture they had kicked about and tossed aside. Next to him his brother wore sneakers as if for a game of soccer. Saladin stepped back to see his brother whole, to see him react to the odd events of this early morning, and Ali was as Ali had always been, tall with a straight spine, the muscles of his shoulders and chest spread broadly and to great effect. But for his face, everything was the same. Saladin looked carefully at his brother's profile. What was normally solemn or indifferent was stiff now, braced through the mouth and jaw and brows by a cold and ready defiance. Saladin recognized the attitude from moments just before his brother entered a race or a fight or some quick assault. Saladin felt the spit dry in his mouth and the last of sleep left him, as did the last of dreams, wants and plans. Once he was empty and hollow, in swept fear. Fear of the day to come, the single-minded guards, the whispering mullah, of his father, just kissed, and of his own brother beside him, at ease in the chaos. He felt Ali's body pulse with vigor and determination of unknown quantities as he stood silent beside Saladin, tall and strong, like a new rifle loved and cared for and not yet fired.

It fell to their father to read the names over the mosque megaphone. He called out the list and ordered the men to come alone. Without families. For questioning. Arez, the electronics repairman. Babak and Biran, the truck drivers who went back and forth to Turkey and sometimes sold German futbols. Ahmed, the baker famous for his hot-stone bread. Soran who played both the daf and the electric guitar better than anything on the radio . . . Saladin knew them by their sons and their *Salaam* on the street and the occasional smiles if the day was warm or a pretty girl had just passed. They were a little less than strangers, and he could not tell what association they held to bind them together on this list, to bring them all, tired eyed and curious, to the wet square at the center of town where the mullah ordered them to stand in a single line, shoulder to shoulder, and announce themselves. Name. Profession. Last trip over the border. Identity.

Saladin's stomach dropped. He understood now how the men were connected to each other. Each was young. Each was known to travel often to Turkey and Iraq for business or family. Each was a man who, depending on the day, might say he was Kurdish but not Iranian, or Kurdish and Iranian, but never Iranian and Iranian alone. Saladin looked at the sky, as if to see what kind of day this was going to be. The morning clouds had cleared and a clean sun danced brilliantly over the blue tiles of the fountain at the edge of the square. A handful of sparrows perched on the lip of the fountain, and Saladin waited for them to sing, but they flew off as the mullah's questions turned to shouts: Name! Loyalty! The business of your last border crossing!

The eleven men said nothing, and the mullah took quick steps around the line of them and then stood very still next to Saladin's father. In the angry silence Babak spoke. I am Babak. Truck driver. Just yesterday I came from Tiblis with a shipment of flour. You can check my papers, my ID card, my vehicle records.

And? the mullah asked.

I am a Kurd.

The mullah nodded.

Why? Saladin turned to his brother, incredulous. Don't they know?

Ali stared ahead with blank eyes and nodded his head in agreement each time a man answered Kurd.

If that is the Ayatollah's question, then this is the answer.

But . . .

Ali shook his head. Saladin jaan, how long before you understand your own fate? At seventeen you still don't understand that if you are a Kurd, you can never be anything else ... Such a shame ...

The mullah requested a location, *discreet and out of the way*. Saladin and Ali's father named a valley a distance from the town where they had gone to hunt as boys. The old man spent those afternoons showing them the slow ways to walk and fast ways to look so they could find and shoot the grouse that darted through the high grass. When they were old enough, they came back alone to get lost in the maze of old trails that cut through the canyons and kept them trapped in long games of hide-and-seek, build-and-destroy, fight-and-escape. Here, Saladin first felt the strange nature of time, the way hours compressed into seconds and seconds could reach out and stretch into eons by the simple sensations of joy and fear. In these canyons too he learned that brothers, in play and game, could be everywhere and nowhere at once. They were always late home, and when they met their mother's hard glare, Ali could never tell her where they had been, and Saladin could not, no matter how well bribed, explain how the time had passed.

The morning they followed their father and the guards, the mullah and the captured, into the secreted valley, time passed in that same strange way. One moment eleven Kurdish men stood in a huddle, eyes open and hands tied, and the next moment they stood blindfolded, lined up shoulder to shoulder. One moment eleven revolutionary guards stood before them, rifles alongside their legs, and the next instant the soldiers knelt, rifles propped on their shoulders and one eye snapped shut. There was the year of the mullah's walk between the two lines, the decade of their father's cigarette and the eternity Saladin spent mourning his mud-caked shoes.

If there was a keeper of this odd time, it was a young man with two cameras. The photographer moved lightly among them, *snap snap snap*, and would, with his photographs, push the morning out longer than the seconds or minutes or hours it held in actual time. Saladin watched as the photographer took one picture of the line of executioners and one of the line of near dead and another of the wet mud between them.

The mullah stood between the lines like a gray pillar. He said nothing and ran two fingers and a thumb through his thick beard, and after a time everyone stood still and ready and in silence. The mullah dropped his hands and held them open like a book. Then, from empty palms, he read.

This afternoon you have been found guilty for the crimes of firearm trafficking to Kurdish nationalist rebels to the west, a violation of the laws of the Islamic Republic that merits instant execution. As you were under the Shah, violent, aggressive, vainglorious, you have exhibited yourself at the dawn of the Islamic Republic, and we will let your deaths serve as examples to your sons. Let them know the righteous path of the devoted heart lies with the Ayatollah Khomeini, and that all other associations and their subsequent actions are Mozzafir-al-den.

The mullah folded his palms together, steadied his gaze. Then an enormous rage opened in his face just long enough for him to shout, *Atash!* And on that order eleven shots fired out from eleven barrels, as somewhere in the sky, a million threads were cut and the

Kurdish men dropped to the valley floor like puppets, useless and tossed aside.

Saladin's knees shook and his eyes blurred, but he tried not to fall as the men had just fallen. He pushed himself up and forced his ears to place the echoes of gunshots as they bounced back and forth along the high rock walls, *bang bang bang* with the same playful volley of thunder.

In the silence that followed, time stood still for everyone to see what was: A man shot in the head. A man shot just under the eye. A man shot in the neck. A man shot in the chest. Another man shot beneath the collarbone. Another in the forehead. Another in the hand that he held over his heart, blood spouting from the hand and from the heart. A man with a wound to his mouth and blood for words. And at the far end a man shot in the waist, still moving, his mouth beneath the blindfold taking in air, letting out whatever sounds came, his feet most alive, kicking and carving shapes into the thick mud.

The mullah approached the family.

Agha Captain. The pistols. Do you have them?

And his father drew out two pistols, one from his holster on his belt and one from the inside of his jacket.

The mullah did not speak, and in this slow time they stood there, four men and two guns.

The mullah nodded his head in the direction of Saladin and Ali.

It is your turn. We must ensure that the convicted die, it is only humane.

The mullah turned to their father.

If your sons complete this task, we will know all is well. If your sons are cowards, then that is a matter that will not last beyond today.

Their father nodded. With steady hands he lit a cigarette and looked toward the mountains.

Pesar-eh man. We have discussed what you must do, and now you must do it . . . These are complicated times . . .

The mullah continued for him.

Your baba is correct. We must know that there are only devoted men under the Ayatollah. Men devoted to this new Iran and nothing else.

If there were tears, Saladin did not feel them on his face. Like his limp hands and weak knees, his face was out of his control. All his senses had rushed to aid his imagination, which was busy taking stock of a life that ended today, this bright spring morning, at seventeen, before his first sex, before his life as a man, in America, on his own. He saw the gun and his father's fallen face. He saw himself dead on the valley floor. He saw, beneath it all, his dirty shoes and knew that if his life was to take a direction, a step that would continue the days after today until they turned into the days of life where Saladin would be a happy stranger, no longer a brother or a son or a Kurd, all thought must stop. He must not think. Saladin let his mind go blank, and time picked up tremendous speed, and one minute his hand was empty and the next it was full with the gun taken off the palm of a father who looked away. Saladin's weak knees were strong now as he walked out to the line of dead and pointed and aimed and shot four times at dead flesh or wet earth or whatever was near until he stood with a numb hand above the still-live man whose blindfold had slipped off such that he could stare at Saladin, eyes to eyes. It was Babak. The gun fell from Saladin's hand, and with it, time fell off its fast rails and slowed. Saladin heard the shush of the mullah's robes as he paced about Saladin's father and brother, and the fury that rang through his voice.

Captain! What is this mess? Finish your work here! Show me!

The mullah shouted the order once, and the dying man twisted his body and pushed his face and all its agony farther into the mud. Saladin sobbed above him and could not, for all his newfound strength, unlock his eyes to see the scene of a mullah who yelled at a father who wished for his son to kill, simply kill, so that the father could go home, to smoke, to bed, to die. Without Saladin's eyes on it, the movie of this life played out in sound alone, and Saladin heard his father clear his throat.

Ali. It is just as we do to the pigeons who cannot fly, to the goats who break their legs. It is God's kindness. Take the gun. So it can be finished.

And with that all time opened up and generations rushed between father and son. Great-grandfathers from the beginning of their bloodline and unborn great-grandsons from far into the future roamed around the first man of these mountains who willed to make a son, to keep a son alive for the sake of more sons.

I will not. Not for you. Not for this Khomeini. It is against my blood. Ali's voice had no tone.

Ali jaan. Do you love this land?

His father asked with cold control.

Yes, Baba. More than you.

Then do as they ask. Do it for the shape of this new country, to tell the new Ayatollah that the Kurds are loyal. Or put us all in danger, the Kurds, me, your brother, these mountains. Ali, take the gun, or forget it all, your home, your sisters, your life as a man here. I will tell the town to forget my first son.

The dying man panted in steady, even breaths. The bullet hole just above his hip surged blood, and Saladin stared at the great red life as it spilled out of him. He imagined himself reaching down to press into the open wound and save the life, but never bent to do it, never had a chance to stain his hand. A close shot blistered the silence, then another and a third. Saladin waited for his own blood to pour, for a pain to sear him, but all that came was the weak spasm of a kick from the dying man, and Ali's fast, strong hand and ready shout.

Come! Come on!

There was a sharp jerk to Saladin's shoulder and arm, and he felt his brother's straight, fast pull and his feet coming unstuck from the mud.

Bodo! Hurry!

Time ran quickly and the brothers ran alongside it, one moment clamoring over the next so what was true seconds ago—Saladin stuck in the mud, the not-dead man as Ali's hands wrapped around a pistol, shooting at the guards until three fell—was now past, and the new truth was Saladin and Ali, hand in hand, away from the bodies and quickly behind the closest boulders and then quickly through a tight crevasse so narrow they ran single file and became boys again, one fast in front of the other, escaping some storied force of death or dishonor that hunted them on the valley floor.

Behind them the story went like this: a furious mullah yelled at guards who were young again, inept and afraid and unable to give proper chase or load spent rifles or fire at the brothers who were now gone, sucked deeply into the veins of trails unchanged since their childhood days.

Behind them a father was kicked to the ground, a boot to his chest, no words off his lips.

Behind them a send-off party of murderers.

Not once did Saladin look back, hopeful for the music, dancing or well-wishes, but took the only celebrations available: the life in his lungs, his fast feet and, far ahead, the lacy chirp of birds. Saladin ran toward their song and then ran faster so to see them, so to know that somewhere in the high, happy calls, it was just as he'd planned it, the lift of his soul after takeoff, the lightness, the fated escape.

The fate of escape.

Days, weeks, maybe months later, the fate of Saladin's escape is to be failed by his feet. The same feet that rushed the brothers up and out of the valley, fold and trip beneath him. He stumbles down the steep tongue of the cargo plane like a fool. Cocooned against the cold hull for seven? twelve? fifteen? hours, his body is crumpled and sore. When he reaches the tarmac, there is relief in the flat concrete and the hot, bright air. Jeeps and hangars and winged machines are all around him, but not one sign of welcome. Nothing says California. Los Angeles. Welcome, Saladin. And for these first minutes it is his fate to wonder, *Have I arrived? Where have I arrived to?* This is not how it he planned it, the end of all running and the beginning of home.

He shouts up into the dark hull of the cargo plane, Ali! Ali! Come out! We're here.

Nothing answers and nothing moves. From underneath the cockpit a man approaches and shouts out, *Hey!* Then once more, with a quicker step: *Hey!* Saladin waves at him as if he belongs here and walks away from the plane, and he is running now, running again, easily and familiarly, from these past weeks. He passes oil trucks and netted boxes of freight and empty buildings and eventually runs in the direction of a far fence and the empty street beyond it. Just as it was in the valley, it is here, and the fate of escape is to never look back, for fear of the man who chases you, for fear your brother is not right behind.

SAFE HOUSES

WE GO TO the borderlands of the west and south where the mountains are inlaid with villages that exist outside of time. Here, we are met by men and women that know only what they know and consider one passing stranger to be as good or bad as the next.

These are the mountain towns that lead us out—to Diyarbakir and Ankara or Islamabad—the stops before the start where we, the strangers, are dropped off by one arrangement and told with little reassurance to wait for the next arrangement to come.

Tomorrow. After dark. A Datsun truck. The driver's name is Ali Reza. Make sure his name is Ali Reza. I think he has a thin mustache. Anyone else is the patrol. After you are certain it is Ali Reza, pay him the rest of what you owe and he will take you across the border. God willing.

The arrangement provides no other advice and leaves us at the edge of villages, in small squares, at the doors of houses that are promised to be safe. Until that tomorrow there is today and tonight, and we have no place to be, nothing to do but worry and wait. A few minutes and a thousand fears pass, and in time something opens—a door, a mouth, the palm of a hand—and we are taken in and treated as if it were always known, as if we had spent the whole of our lives in this nameless spot.

We are fed, offered a mat and a flat pillow and left alone to drink tea, smoke cigarettes and fret. If the house has small children, they approach and watch our new presence, openly curious about the soft luggage, the fancy shoes, the digital wristwatches. They keep close to our wonders while their parents keep a distance. No questions are asked of affiliations, circumstance or destination. Everything has already been explained to them by the smugglers; all arrangements have been made.

Yes.

The men and women say, for a little bit of money they will lie during the weekly inspections of their homes and schools and mosques.

Yes.

They will keep us warm, feed us as best they can. *Yes*, for a little bit of money they will upset their lives and hide their young wives and oldest daughters from these fleet-footed strangers without homes or futures.

Yes. For a little bit of money, befaymin.

Night comes and we sit with the men and women of the village. They are quiet. To soothe ourselves we talk, beseech God, try to explain.

I was halfway along life's path, ay Khoda, you must understand this is not how it was planned.

I had a position at the university.

I was a second administrator at the TV station.

I just received my certificate to practice dentistry.

I was in love.

In school.

Engaged.

Now what? Three months have passed and the country is already falling apart. I am an Islamic man, just like you, but this regime is like a black hand over our faces, his picture, his komiteh guards, are everywhere, as bad as SAVAK. My own uncle was taken to prison for refusing to take off his tie. My cousin took twenty lashes to the soles of his feet for holding his girlfriend's hand, for refusing to call her a slut in front of the police. My brother-in-law, my next-door neighbor, my father, my mother, missing for weeks . . .

We tell of the last time and the time before that and how this escape is the choice.

I had to go. What else was there to do?

In dim rooms we tell these things to the men and women of villages that have no before and no after, where no person has stood before another person and said, And now we are in the era of King so-and-so, and now we are in the era of Shah so-and-such and next year his son will rule over us. For their part they sit quietly, take their tea and are careful not to look at our sad, scurrying eyes and keep their ears tuned outside, to the sounds of the wind.

In the morning we awake tired from the night's unwieldy dreams and stare absently into the wide eyes of children who toss us a ball, a half-knit sweater, a crayon, a smile. Exhausted, we stare back, and soon we are touching the child's hand, tossing the ball, enjoying the hot tea and the warmth of a hearth that did not fade in the night. From the kitchen we are enticed by the smells of onions, saffron and grilled meats, and under our feet a rug with worn patterns pleases our eyes. Suddenly, there is comfort. Comfort to make the will soft, the knees feeble, comfort to change the mind.

The villagers notice our sudden calm, the way we look about and consider their warm homes and quiet lives. They remind us.

Go, go, now, take some fresh air while you wait. The camion will be here any minute.

We have forgotten ourselves.

Yes. Of course. I must not miss the camion, of course. I must leave immediately.

And we do as we are told even if we don't know why. When the arrangement comes, it is a truck or a small van. Maybe it is a pack of mules saddled heavy with blankets or a broad-chested man who carries the complete skins of sheep, heads included, and issues only one instruction.

Wear this. Yes, the head over your head. Cover your shoulders and walk on your hands and knees. But slowly. They patrol from the air now. Remember, move slowly, sheep have no reason to run.

We tune our hearts to a frequency somewhere between empty and intrepid and forget the child, the rug, the tea, and move on. There are no farewells, and like that we come and go from these border villages. Years later, in the new country, we will remember that awkward escape, the flavor of the khoresht we ate that night, the color of the child's asking eye. These memories can't be controlled. They grow and fade and harass us in dreams and waking life the same.

Behind us, in the villages without time, there is no memory.

In our wake there is no talk of where to or why or when, and the men and women of the villages resume their life, undisrupted. The cycles of seasons, sex, birth, planting, harvest and death come and go. Only the children, for whom the cycles are not yet set, still fascinate on the appearance and disappearance of birds and butterflies. They run to ask those who know, But why? Why do they stop in our hyatt? Why do they leave?

Those who know ask back.

Are there flowers in your hyatt? Are the flowers in your hyatt fragrant?

Yes.

Are they colorful and beautiful?

Yes.

Are the walls of your hyatt tall and safe?

Yes.

In the villages without time the children wait only so long for understanding to come.

FIRST NIGHTS

IT IS NOT as he imagined, this Los Angeles, the America on the other side of the fence, and Saladin walks away from the airport with quick steps, hungry for some sign to convince him he has arrived—a nice car, women in short skirts and lipstick, a sandy beach—anything to welcome him as California's newest son.

He walks through an area of no end. The buildings are low-slung and the streets are dirty and without life, and it is no different from the anonymous outskirts of Ankara, Istanbul, and Tabriz. The similarity makes him nervous, nervous that he is lost and nervous that he has failed, and his feet pick up as much speed as they can and soon he is running, a fast step for every line he mutters beneath his breath. *I have come. Where have I come? I have come? Where have I come?* Beyond the flat rooftops he sees mountains, shorter than the mountains he has known, but green and near. He sees their dry dirt and dusty shrubs, and somewhere among them a clutter of wooden letters spells

HOLLYWOOD, high and white. Saladin anchors himself in their direction and moves on.

He comes to a street full of traffic, people and sound. Lights tell the cars where to move, and lights tell the people when to stop and when to go. Tiredness overwhelms him but he crosses streets and intersections and pushes himself up one block after another, glad for the sight and sounds of flesh, for the eyes that catch his to say, *Yes, you are alive, you are here*, and nothing more. He keeps on even when he would most like to stop and sit and stare at the strange new faces, bodies, skins, clothes and moods, all of them incompatible and odd. But he goes on, forces himself to keep walking, to be alone as they are alone, to move like the men move, with purpose, on the way from one place to the next.

In the middle of the next block Saladin is forced to stop. In front of him a man and a woman are intertwined, their limbs tangled, faces fastened at the mouth, hooked, it seems, by the tongues. She is tall with short hair, and he is taller, enough so that he must bend to grab her waist so they can sway, turn their heads back and forth, and never once forgo the lock of their lips. Saladin stands rooted to the concrete, and all that moves through them moves through him as well. Never has he seen such a thing. Not on the street, not at school, not between his mother and father, only in the cinema, and then again and again until each film became the long wait for the kiss and nothing else.

Cars and people pass but Saladin is stuck, as if between the bodies of the couple, and watches them pull near and nearer into each other, and heat fills the hollows of his groin and stomach and chest and throat and fumes up into the heavy hollow of his head, burns just one degree hotter and ignites. Here! On the street! Saladin turns to share the excitement with his brother.

Ali! Can you believe it? On the street! Only in America! Ali! Ali?

But his brother is not at his side. The block has emptied. Behind him there is only a shopping cart pushed into the curb, in front of him a scarred, squat palm. Where is his brother? Saladin remembers exactly where his brother is and moves, quickly now, so he might forget. The same fast feet eat up the sidewalk to keep hysteria back, and he steps briskly and practices. *My name is . . . It is nice to meet you. Yes. I am from Italy. I am from Greek. I am twenty-six years old. I am twenty-seven years old. Hello. Tomorrow is my birthday, I will be twenty-nine years! Old enough for America. A brother? No, I have no brother. Not a one. You are a mistake.* He corrects himself. *You are a mistaken. I am happy to meet you.*

It works, and after a time the exertion pushes the memories back and he begins to see the city around him, a city he recognizes from a lifetime of films, a city that could be no other, with the tall buildings of clean glass and bending palms and a golden sunlight that touches everything. He looks to the sun itself, brighter here than it was in the mountain town, closer, more brilliant, and knows it as it is known everywhere: to rise in the east and set in the west. That knowledge snaps through Saladin like a reflex, and with certainty he can tell the cardinal points and thinks back to a map of America that showed a country between two oceans, one east and one west, and like that he knows how he will be welcome, how he can finally arrive. Saladin looks for a western street, long and straight, where the sun drops down, so he can follow it all the way to the great water that ends Los Angeles, a city with half her letters in the sea.

He arrives at the beach just after dusk, and the expanse of blue water is, in shade and spread, the same as the sky. Sand fills the cracks in his leather shoes, and Saladin walks until he is at the lip of her, thick with white froth, and walks until he is in, ankles, knees and thighs, still clothed and moving like a man in a trance. The water is as salty as his own tears and it is warm; water like a meal and a medicine; a tonic in which to bathe and receive the ablution that blesses the Kurd boy, poor boy, new boy. It rises over his hip and then to the elbows and neck, and then he is entirely under, where the long tongues of strong currents lick him in a wild love fiercer than any caress he has ever known. Tight in the mouth of the sea he is anonymous, a body cast out, kissed. He dives down to where the blue becomes black, a whole darkness where the only sensation is the sting of salt as it cuts through the last embraces, last looks, of that old life. Saladin stays under until breathless, convulsing, and clean.

It is a long bath.

He swims and is sure to keep sight of the beach, the land, this continent he has come to, and when the excitement is too much, he swims to it and walks onto shore like the first offered man, the boy from before dissolved now into particles smaller than sand, smaller than the oncoming evening mist, smaller than the air itself.

The wet clothes stick to him but he feels nothing of their cling and lies his body down on the sand. Above, the sky is made of dark and light blues and he imagines the colors are blankets he can, if he wants, pull across himself from the old world into the new.

This is here.

He says to himself.

This is here. There is no forward and no return, and Saladin is happy, caught between this coming night and days of dreams he has dragged halfway across the earth.

Sleep does not come. All around the beach has been dark for hours but Saladin cannot calm his body, electric and stiff and packed with energy as if it were morning or midday or the seconds just after a nightmare. He tries to remember the start of this day and can only think of dawn on the island, and even that seems like one thousand years ago. There was a brief, almost miniature night on the plane and this is the first night after that, but Saladin cannot for sure say how this day connects them. Is this the same day he left the island or a different day? And if so, how many different days have passed in between? He waits to sense the clock in his body, but it has turned off in confusion. Saladin hugs his knees in close and wishes for some sunlight to illuminate this world and match his ready mood. This is the second night he will see all the way through.

The first night he saw all the way through was the night of the day the brothers ran out of the valley and up into the mountains, until they could no longer run and had to walk, Ali ahead and Saladin behind. It was a night without sleep, bed, father, home. There was little to discuss, every direction was up, away from the trees and grass and hearths they knew and into the rocks and sky. They walked in silence. By evening Saladin could no longer see his brother and had to listen for the faint lead of steps that padded out in front of him as night took his brother's body, the shape of boulders and the outlines of summits all around.

Until the dark came, Saladin moved with a hurry made partly of fright and partly from the rush of memories that came off the land as they mixed this escape with the childish games from before. Just as before, he followed his brother's back up the trails and over the passes where their boyhood selves had played as wealthy traders, fleet messengers for a king, warriors en route to battle. Ali, the older, always kept ahead, but they would walk down together, as victors, worldly explorers, new grooms just back from collecting twin brides who sat split-legged atop invisible horses while the brothers argued which was the finer. *Mine sings like Maman. Yes, but mine has the sound of gold in her laugh.* And they were always out of the mountains by dusk. Saladin had never seen night so far from home, had never slept in a bed that was not his own. He ran to catch his brother.

Ali, where are we going?

Away.

Where?

Where it is safe. To hide for a week, maybe two. Until the mullah leaves and we can go back and fight.

Fight? Fight what?

Today was a bad day for the Kurds . . . we must . . . we will stay away for a time, a week, maybe two, and then sneak back. Ehyd's brother will keep us in his house.

And tonight? Where are we going to stay tonight?

Nowhere. We are going to walk.

Where? Where are we going to sleep?

The footsteps stopped.

Saladin jaan. Am I not your older brother?

Yes.

Then listen to me. You must follow me. Don't you remember the stories the old men told? Kurds have always escaped through these mountains. We are no different. Even you, you who have lived in the cinema, you are no different. We will follow in their footsteps and there will be a place to stay, a place to hide for a few weeks and then we can go home. With honor, for honor.

The moon was no more than an eyelash in the sky and lent little light to the land. Of his brother's face, Saladin could only make out shiny teeth and the lively whites of eyes. Soon there was no face and no brother, and the same fast footsteps padded out into the dark. Saladin ran to keep up, and like this they passed through the darkness, their faint chalky shadows jaunty in front of them, and then alongside, and then behind and then gone.

They spent the morning in descent. Shaky talus slides gave way to hilly gravel roads that gave way to a hot, rolling piedmont that they walked with aching knees and a hunger that went unmentioned. When Saladin saw them, the six or seven men who rose and sank in the high grains, he stepped forward to call out, *I am hungry. Do you have food? We are hungry.*

But Ali held him back.

Wait. Wait.

The brothers stood out of sight, and Ali studied the dusty men, their dip and pull and rise and tie, told Saladin to wait until they found a rhythm and logic in the work so when they approached with their *Hello, we are traveling through, is there a place for the night in exchange for a few days' work?* the men were not interrupted and responded easily.

Yes, Baba, yes. Come help.

The work was easy to learn and Saladin copied his brother to stretch and pull and gather and knot the hay. Ali only spoke to him once, when they were both hidden beneath the high level of the grains.

If they ask, say we are going to Tabriz. For exams.

Otherwise they worked quietly like the others, and when the field was flat, they followed the oldest man into a village of mud-and-straw huts, chickens and skinny goats. The old man washed his head with clean water from a ceramic gourd. When the water was cloudy, he handed the bowl to Saladin and smiled, dust still lodged in the creases of his face. The brothers cleaned as well as they could, Ali with serious determination, as if washing for prayer. Saladin watched him work with the dirty water and saw all the sweat of the last day and night and day stick to his face like a wet glaze.

Inside the hut a woman in a sequined scarf crouched beside a smoky fire. She did not rise to greet them. Across the room the old man had taken his seat and busied himself with the filling and lighting and smoking of a pipe he did not offer. When the food came, it was gelid and salted and held the flavor of the dust that coated everything. Out of habit Saladin tasted the food and then forced himself to swallow without chewing and fed his hunger as best he could. Ali ate with relish, and the old man paid no attention to either of them. When he finished, he gathered his bones up and stood, burped and walked slowly out of the room. Ali casually asked after him.

Have you heard the news?

News?

Of the Shah? The Ayatollah? The old news.

The old man rubbed his groin and the smell of him filled the small room, and Saladin could no longer even swallow and pushed his plate toward the old lady, who watched everything with the one eye left uncovered by the shawl.

Baba jaan, there is always some new king. Here, there, what do I know?

The old man stepped outside and they heard the sound of a thin stream of piss. Ali followed and left Saladin alone with the old woman. No longer shy, she turned her uncovered face to him. She had no nose, only flatness with two uneven holes just above the lip, and Saladin stumbled out of the hut in a shocked and childish rush.

His brother and the old man were crouched together near the ground. The old man picked through his teeth with a stalk of grain.

Then you know nothing of the news? Of the massacres, the revolutionary guards who have been shot . . .

Ack. Shahs come and shahs go. Here nothing changes, thanks be to God.

Ali looked at Saladin as he smiled and repeated the words of the old man.

Yes. Thanks be to God.

They stayed outside a while longer, and Saladin listened for a television or a radio, but there was only the susurration of the wind through the grain and some far, loud bug. A few smoky wisps rose from the center of the huts, but no lights flickered from the glassless windows, no sound of machine or music came into the street, and Saladin understood. In a town without news there is no news of them, their crime, their flight, and without news they were simply brothers on a journey, innocents.

Ali turned a shaft of grain between his teeth.

Yes. Yes. Nothing changes. Thanks be to God.

They worked days in the field, and nights they returned to the old man's hut, ate the woman's bland food, and slept through the quiet dark. Sleep did not come easily. If it was not the old woman's snoring and the old man's restlessly chattering teeth, then it was the deep silence that covered the village and seeped into all the homes and heads. Saladin lay awake remembering the lyrics of Elvis songs, lines from James Bond movies, the particular pitch of radio static that hummed behind the Voice of America. But the quiet was bigger than these small memories and he stayed awake, craving some hum of the world outside this world. In the silence he felt the dust of the village seep into his fingernails, between his eyelids, up the crack of his ass as if the earth were trying to bind him. Even the sky pressed him down until he could barely breathe, and in this suffocation came sleep.

Each night he dreamed about his mother.

In one dream he was a boy in his third year of school. His mother had just died and he was asked to give a report about her. He stood before the class in his wool V-neck sweater and short pants and read from a piece of paper that was written in her hand. *I had a mother once. When she slept on her side, the weight of one breast made a line down the middle of her chest, like she had been folded in half. In the morning she drank dark tea and did not look anywhere but at her magazine and the bottom of her teacup and never at my father, who shouted loud enough to shake the windows. At night she smoked thin cigarettes and sang or cried or laughed, depending on the moon, she said. I had a mother who loved cinema and radio programs and me more than my brother. A mother who took me to my first cinema and the one after and gave me money to go by myself. I had a mother who stood far apart from my father, called him a coward, a weak captain, a man who could not provide for his family or send her to Tehran to buy clothes and see cinema. And then one day I had no mother and a father who was not as sad as I.*

In the mornings Saladin was the last to wake and trailed behind the men on their way to the fields as Ali went up ahead with the rest, addressed the village wives and children by name, while the women smiled kindly in return. No one noticed the surly brother who ambled and squinted just behind.

On the fourth day they did not go to the fields. The men woke and ate and washed but did not walk west as they had all the days before and turned east instead, in the direction of the hills from which Saladin and Ali had just fled. Ali grabbed the old man by his thin arm.

The fields? Why aren't we going to the fields?

The old man shook off the hold and kept walking.

We have duties beyond those fields. Come.

★ ★ ★

After an hour of walking they stopped on the side of a slope where the air blew hot and they were without shadow and exposed. Around them small mounds rose from the ground, and where there were no mounds, the earth gaped with deep, square holes. Saladin bent to look into one and saw the dirt wink with tiny blue, green and gold eyes. The men went to work, with fingertips and tiny tools, and carved away the earth little by little. When a jewel or ornament dropped into their open palm, they tossed it into a basket with all the ceremony given to a bulb of garlic or blossom of radish. The old man came to the brothers with a small shovel and an even smaller pickax.

Carefully. Very carefully.

In the tight space the brothers dug back-to-back, and Saladin felt every move of Ali's shoulder and torso against his own. In front of him the walls of dirt twinkled with all manner of tiny buttons and medallions, charms and broken trinkets, but Saladin could find no worth in them.

How long until we leave this place, Ali? We can't stay forever.

Behind him Ali's back and shoulders moved relentlessly and answered, breathless.

Baba, relax. This place is good for now. We have to stay away for a while.

How long?

Longer. Until the news of the guards is gone. Until the mullah leaves our town.

There was nowhere to go, nowhere to fight or argue, the hole was small and with the energy of his anger Saladin could only dig. When the pieces started to fall, he threw them up without care for their shine or shape, and soon his face and neck were covered in sweat. He felt Ali's shoulders jostle up and down, and then he heard his brother laugh.

Just like your pool. Remember? The pool you wanted so badly. The one we dug in the backyard?

Eleven years old, their mother just dead, Saladin lived in the cinema. He went for the dark, the sounds and the images of a world lovely and clean, full of mothers and wives and happy girls. In many of the movies there were pools. Rectangles of clean water and tile, and every time there was a pool there were pretty girls in swimsuits, men with jokes, sun and splashing. He begged his father to build one in their hyatt. *Build it yourself,* he had said, and Saladin bribed his brother with the money he had saved for a trip to Tehran. Ali took the money but was of little help. He would throw shovel loads of dirt over his shoulder onto Saladin and joke, *You don't think Haleh is going to put on a swimsuit to get into this puddle? Does Haleh even have a swimsuit?* Saladin ignored him and the hole grew bigger, and Saladin imagined the crystalline water, the swimming races, the ghost of his mother smiling down at her beautiful reflection. His brother left him on his own and the fall rains came, and in the end it was a shallow, muddy hole that even their youngest sister, a toddler who loved puddles, refused to get in. Ali went on, giggling.

Saladin did not get annoyed now, tried not to get frustrated that he was stuck, again, in a hole with his brother, he did not even hear him, so quickly and noisily did his head jump from memory to memory all the way to the idea that made him dig furiously at a large piece packed tightly in the earth. The pools were in America.

He had not wanted the pool, he had wanted America. A country to the west of the mountain town, far, impossible to see except in the cinema. And now, even in this hole, Saladin is a dozen steps closer to America. All of the hardest and heaviest steps, the ones out of the mountain town, out from under the heavy press of love and family, name and blood, had already been taken the night they did not sleep, and all the steps now, out of the hole, west, across land and water, would be far easier.

What if we don't go back? If we keep going?

His brother laughed.

Where should we go, dear Saladin of the Ayyubids? Conqueror of the western lands. Where do we go with no money and no family?

Saladin ignored the joke and picked gently at the buried form. The earth was loosening her grasp, and Saladin could see a hoof, bent at the knee.

To a city. With electricity. And cars. We could hide in Istanbul. Hamid's brothers went. He said the girls don't cover and half of them have blond hair. And there is a cinema on every other corner . . .

Beya Baba! Istanbul! What do you know about Istanbul? They put their Kurds in prison for speaking Kurdish there! With what money do you plan to live in Istanbul?

Saladin had nothing to say against these charges. He dug with greater force and finally the earth let go. The figurine of a goat, solid weight, entirely of gold. The face was complete with details: thin lips, wide eyes and a stern jaw, horns erect, precise. He rubbed it in his hand a few times but could not hold back the excitement of this omen, this sign from the ground itself. He held the goat up in front of Ali's face.

Ali, look. This is the money that will take us to Istanbul. It is gold. It can take us even farther.

Ali grabbed the goat and put it in his mouth, and because there was no room in the hole, the brothers fought sloppily with much grabbing and screaming, and soon the other men came to watch and laugh at the boys wrapped around each other like snakes. They raised them out and chided.

In our village a brother doesn't fight his brother.

Ali spit the goat out and handed it to the old man, who rubbed off the saliva and nodded at the sight of the steady horns and even face.

Aufareen.

He passed the figurine to Saladin.

Here. Our news today, our news tomorrow, the news from one thousand years ago.

That night the village ate together outside. A lamb roasted on a large iron spit, and a young girl walked from man to woman to man and offered honey candies. She wore no scarf and her hair was the color of the high grains and fell just below her waist. She sat between the brothers on a bench they shared by the fire.

I am the beekeeper. I must stay to keep the bees.

They took pieces of her candy and the brothers nodded and sucked as sweetness flooded their mouths, the flavor of every clover for miles.

Ali faced her.

May I have another piece?

The girl obliged and held out the tray. Ali placed the candy in his mouth and smiled. She offered Saladin the sweets on her tray and he refused.

Ali, we should leave soon. We should leave now. Our time here is done. We have our gold . . . no one knows our names yet, but tomorrow they might . . .

Saladin watched Ali take in his demand and then look at the girl. A gold-haired wife. A return down the mountains with a gold-haired wife, split-legged, atop a horse, singing. They had known the fantasy since they were boys.

Saladin, relax. I am the one who has done wrong. Not you. Wait here with me for a week more and we will return together, and I will fight and you can hide in the cinema. It is not for me to judge that we are different. Maman and Baba always said . . .

For courage Saladin caressed the prize in his pocket. He let his fingers run across the eyes, the stiff legs, the pressed and stubborn face.

Boshe. I will go by myself. You go back to that town to die and I will go the other way.

Saladin turned away from the fire, the roasted lamb, the honey candies and walked out from the village of silence and wind. He pulled the last of the honey sweetness from his cheeks and kept his fist tight around the body of the goat and promised himself to walk until he came to a highway full of cars, storefronts full of radios. When he reached the gravel road that had brought them to the village, he heard Ali's breath and his light footsteps fall in behind his own.

Okay. Okay. Maybe you are right. Maybe one village away will be safer. What difference does it make as long as we can walk our steps back home? Inshallah.

The words meant nothing to Saladin, and he let his ears fill with the permission in his brother's voice, the hard love and hope. He walked forward, fast and ahead.

EMPTY DAYS MADE OF HEAT

IN THE HOURS just before dawn Saladin falls asleep on the beach; sand blanket, sand bed.

When he wakes, the surf is farther away, pulled down from his feet like sheets left behind by a risen bedmate. The air is full of fog and his body is stiff from the chill of wet clothes and the cool night. Beside his head, bugs jump into and out of the sand, their long, thin forms quick with a logic Saladin, half-awake, cannot make out. He looks beyond them into the thick, blue mist where there are people. Two girls walk hand in hand, heads thrown back, laughing. A tall, thin man moves a flat-bottomed plate tenderly across the sand. Now and again the plate beeps, now and again the man crouches, smells the sand and digs. Closer, a boy of Saladin's age stretches out in a posture of easy relief. He wears a knitted sweater and a thick winter cap and keeps a bottle close at hand. Saladin does not know the names of these other citizens and cannot call to them in greeting or query, and exhaustion comes over him again, thick and heavy. He puts his head to the damp sand and curls until a coal of warmth heats in his center and he can sleep. After a time the man with the metal detector reaches him. He runs the plate over Saladin. Nothing buzzes, nothing beeps.

When he wakes again, it is under the glare of a fierce sun. His shirt and pants are baked on now; along with the sand and sweat, the stiffness of his salty clothes aggravates his collar and crotch. He stands to shake it out, and his muscles and bones and clothes break open this thin, new sandy shell and Saladin moves like a crab—quickly, angrily, sideways—to the sea. The ocean is calm with small waves that break on themselves, and he takes his shoes off, rolls up his pants and walks in. The water is crisp and pulls down and out the heat of panic that spreads through and over him, panic of a man without a place in the world. He lets his feet sink down into the wet sand, a little deeper with every wave.

He looks at the shore of America.

The wide beach is spotted with families and people lying down alone. A few children play in the water, and a mother is always close by, with a towel, a shovel or a bucket, and Saladin cannot look at the mothers for too long without thinking of his own mother, her wish to spend a day at the sea. He looks back to the sand where people arrange themselves in little colonies of blankets and umbrellas and low metal chairs. They are not as lively as he imagined. There are no boys with guitars and hand drums and no girls dancing. It is a quiet morning at the beach, no more, no less. He looks beyond, to the long wooden boardwalk where people walk and run and roll in front of an endless string of stores whose windows advertise postcards and sunglasses and inflated toys. Some of the men and women wear their swimming suits like regular clothes, and this is an encouraging detail, a reminder that his life is going as planned. It may not be the beach as he knows it from movies, but it is sunny and the people are happy and the people are tan and near naked. He washes his hands and face and arms, pulls his feet up and out of the sand and walks back to shore, where he dries quickly, tucks and buttons his shirt, and moves toward the boardwalk, toward this first day of his Los Angeles life.

On the boardwalk Saladin steps into a heavy traffic of children on roller skates and men on short boards with wheels and old woman on bicycles. He moves in spurts and tries not to get hit, but it is difficult because the more he moves, the more he notices the asses and breasts that are everywhere, offered and ready for all eyes. The traffic shouts at him.

Hey!

Watch out!

And he jumps and runs from one side of the sunny walk to another. The girls are alone and in groups, dressed in two pieces that cover their breasts and bottoms and little more. Some of them wear short dresses, and some wear cutoff jeans but no shirts. And Saladin cannot stop himself from staring as they pass. He wants badly to talk to a girl, to talk so that one might smile and he might feel the skin she shows, but they move past him without so much as a half glance. A group of dancers perform against a rail, and Saladin stops to watch and gather himself. They are black skinned and young and they fold and unfold to the angry, fast beats that play from a machine that is not plugged in. One of the dancers offers him a hat and Saladin sees that it is full of coins and folded bills, and he shakes his head and moves back into the flow of smiling old women and hairless, muscular men and laughing girls who move their tongues around ice creams and straws and their own lips, and Saladin walks in a bliss of disbelief. He tries to do as they do, to pay no mind to the fantasy all around, and walks straight and with a stiff neck, pulled up and on by the hot, bright sun, and soon he feels as if he has been walking like this for a long time. It is as if this stride on the California boardwalk is no more than a continuation of the steps he and Ali took away from the honey maiden, steps that led them into a lonely, blank dawn and a hot, empty day.

For the rest of the night the brothers did not speak. At sunrise Saladin still marched ahead, keeping direction as if they had a destination, a place they were expected to be. Behind him Ali moved slower and stopped now and again to look about the wide land and wonder if that was a village over there and maybe they should stop and stay. Saladin said little, only enough to quiet his brother and buy himself more silence. As long as the villages were small and without power, he knew they had to keep going, move on to some place of noise and light. By noon they were in a desolate land without even one village to tempt them to rest or to take shade from the sun that pushed into the crowns of their heads like dull daggers.

When the first car, a yellow Paykan, slowed and the man leaned his head out the passenger window and shouted:

A ride?!

Saladin easily broke his stride and ran to the car, shouting back at his brother with a volume and force he had wanted to use all day:

Ali, come on! Quick! Let's go!

The driver introduced himself as the older brother, and the passenger agreed.

Of course I am the younger. And more handsome.

From what Saladin could see the two shared no features. The driver was dark and balding, round over the cheeks and shoulders, and his brother the passenger was fair skinned and sharp featured with yellow hair that spiraled out from his head in huge curls. After the introductions the car began to move, and Ali looked darkly at Saladin and pushed himself between the driver and the passenger.

Excuse me for asking . . .

Ali cleared his throat and the voice that came out was boyish and high. We are grateful for your kind offer. But my brother and I are only going a short distance.

No one listened and no one answered. The passenger brother was busy twisting the radio knob over patches of broken static cut through with the sound of news. He tuned until the broadcast played clearly and the voice of a news anchor sounded out, calm and proud.

Today riots in Shiraz brought out ten thousand . . . A Jewish merchant was arrested and then shot for resisting arrest . . . No word has been issued from the Shah, who remains in exile in Egypt. There are reports of a grave physical illness . . . Outside the city of Kermanshah three revolutionary guards have been injured by renegade Kurdish rebels thought now to have escaped to the mountains of the west. The Ayatollah urges citizens to come forth with any information about the rebels. Detractors of any kind are considered a grave threat, and the Ayatollah reminds us that the peace of the republic is in our hands. Thanks be to Allah. The most merciful. Khodafez.

The passenger brother switched off the radio and answered back.

Van. We are going to Van. Where are you two going?

Ali pushed himself back into the seat, and Saladin watched as in seconds his brother was replaced by a ghost, a spirit of fear and nerves, pale faced and covered in a thin sweat. Ali cleared his throat again, and Saladin saw the node in Ali's neck pulse as it would in a child that swallows again and again, so as not to cry.

We are going to Van too. We too. Us too. To Van. For exams.

The passenger brother looked at the driver, who nodded once slowly, then spoke.

Very convenient. Do you have papers?

Saladin and Ali remained silent.

It's no matter. The border is no problem. We do it all the time. The car has Turkish plates and our mother lives just on the other side, and we are doing nothing more than going to Friday lunch. She lives in one of those old towns, older than old, famous for its crumbling Mongol castle. Hoscap Palace. There is nothing to the crossing, the passenger brother reassured them, his golden curls bouncing around his eyes and jaw. It is simple. I tell the guards the same joke every time. I say, yes, yes, I realize we've been back and forth a number of times in the last few months, but what can we do? Our dear maman would die if we did not make it to Friday lunch. One o'clock exactly. What would she do without her four most beloved sons? God bless her, mother of twelve. She was here long before these silly borders. How do you expect an angel like that to understand?

The passenger brother laughed at his old joke and repeated bits of it beneath his breath. Next to him the driver brother squinted at Saladin in the rearview mirror.

Can you believe that stupid joke works every time? Imagine . . .

They arrived in Tabriz as the city woke from the afternoon nap. The streets filled with men and women on their way to shops or to work. At a busy intersection a revolutionary guard stopped every other car to search the insides and interrogate the drivers. Women in chadors flapped past women in skirts and makeup and each cast back their mean kohl stares. Saladin watched flocks of mullahs move in loud, confident groups and large banners of Khomeini swayed from every available banister, railing and light pole. So many images of the same man. There had been only one image of the Shah, the same one that hung in his father's barracks, at the school, in the lobby of the cinema, but this new Khomeini came in a dozen faces: ashen against a gray backdrop that spelled PROGRESS; colorful in a photograph that showed him receiving flowers from a young child; heavy lidded and severe before a field of tulips, the word FREEDOM spelled atop his turban. He never smiled and his seriousness seemed to come from everywhere and nowhere all at once.

They parked the car in an alley beside the bazaar, and the driver and the passenger brothers got out and stretched, spoke quietly to each other and smoked cigarettes. Saladin and Ali waited in the car, and when the brothers were done talking, the younger opened Saladin's door and asked:

Well? Are you waiting for the servants to do it?

The driver brother insisted they eat at a certain kabobi and then take their tea at a particular teahouse and smoke at yet another teahouse and on and on, one after the next, each more delicious than before. The lights of the town had come on and the streets were busy, the glass of the restaurants and teahouses fogged and dripping. Saladin could not help but enjoy himself. Somehow his life was instantly different. What was confined before, by rules and family and a life of familiarity, was let loose and thus possible here. He was in a city, with new friends. He could take tea like a man in a teahouse, smoke like a man with the rest of the men. He could move, if he liked, across a border, away from his childhood and into some great, open unknown. The directions of his life, at this moment, were limitless. Saladin ate greedily and smoked with a fervor, and the tobacco went to his head to make him quick, impatient and crazy.

Ali did not smoke or eat the offered snacks and took every opportunity to ask the brothers.

The border. When do we cross the border? Can you stop just before it? My brother and I can make our own way to Van later ...

The driver grew annoyed.

Eh, baba! Who starts a desert crossing dying of thirst? Drink, drink now and soon enough you will be wishing for water, for the fragrant tea in this lovely teahouse. Relax, we will cross together. No question about it. It is our pleasure to take you.

* * *

At a nearly empty teahouse they were joined by a man in a stiff silk suit who carried a heavy leather satchel. He wore sunglasses with yellow lenses and a gold watch. He sat and ordered no tea and made no small talk. He looked first at Saladin and then at Ali and then back at Saladin and then at Ali again. There were no introductions and the passenger brother began to speak in a low and formal tone. A few revolutionary guards came in, their faces like masks, and sat to drink tea. Saladin tried to ignore them, but the shine of their new boots caught his eye, so similar were they to the boots that marched through his father's barracks yesterday. Or was it the day before? Or was it last week? Or the week before? The stylish man paid no attention to the guards and carried on a reserved conversation with the passenger brother that ended with the question:

Which one will it be?

The passenger pointed to Ali.

This one.

Are you sure?

The stylish man looked at Ali directly and then around him as if at the aura that came off the edges of his skin and hair.

Yes. He is more afraid. More afraid of a mistake.

Very well. There is payment in Ankara. Not before.

The stylish man stood up and left without handshakes or embraces and left behind his heavy leather satchel.

They drove into the night, and no matter how many times Saladin put the satchel on Ali's lap, his brother knocked it off, and after a time Saladin was forced to consider it. What could be of such value to require such precautions? He knew of nothing, aside from gold, or silver perhaps, but the bag was too light. He thought about his father, what he valued most, his uniform, his glass pipes, his opium. His opium. Saladin picked up the bag and smelled through the leather. It smelled of his father's jacket, the thick musk of dirt and sweat and opium locked in the wool. The smell was the same. In an instant Saladin knew the cost of a border crossing, knew that if they were caught at the border, they would be sent to some dank jail cell just like the one their father used to man. He pushed the bag toward his sleeping brother and stared out the window at the night desert that passed, part star, part earth, and stopped himself from thinking too much about what could or could not be.

When he woke, morning light blazed through the front windshield and the driver and passenger brothers shielded their eyes as they argued.

Relax, it's not too late.

No, baba, it is too late. They've already changed shifts. Now we get a fresh guard with nothing to do but search the car.

Na, na. They don't change until later.

Outside the window a man knelt and stood, knelt and stood on a threadbare rug. He wore no shoes and Saladin was surprised he had not found a more private place to pray. Ahead of them he could see a checkpoint, the border, and then Turkey.

Saladin shook Ali by the shoulders.

Posho.

Ali rolled his head to the other side and kept his eyes closed.

Wake up. We are at the border.

When his brother opened his eyes, Saladin saw red veins reached around the pupils in every direction, and a thick, yellow crust had formed at the edges of his eyelids.

Ali. You have to wake up. You have to hold this bag.

You are the one with the hero's name. You do it . . . I am not going to jail for a crime as stupid as smuggling. Come now, Saladin jaan, you wanted to cross the border . . . you take the risk.

Ali closed his eyes and Saladin looked to the front seats. The brothers hadn't heard. Saladin shoved the bag onto Ali's lap and lifted his limp hand over it.

Take it. Remember. They are your books for school.

Ali muttered beneath his breath but could not seem to pull himself out of whatever sleep or dream held him.

The checkpoint was well established and functional, the buildings and roads no older than the young countries they separated. In front of the kiosk a worn flag of Turkey fluttered beside the snapping-new flag of the Islamic Republic. They slowed and then stopped at a gate, a long wooden arm painted yellow and black stopping the cars that tried to pass. An older man in the uniform of a revolutionary guard, beardless and in his own shoes, approached.

Salaam alaikum.

The men exchanged greetings, travel documents, the driver's birth certificate, citizenship papers, their mother's address and dead father's occupation.

The guard looked into the back windows.

So many sons, eh? So close in age? Lucky family.

The passenger brother sighed theatrically.

Baba was a very vigorous man.

The guard walked around the car and tapped twice on the window where Ali's head was pressed and sleeping. The third tap came from the butt of his rifle, and Ali's spine shot up straight.

He rolled the window down and looked up at the guard and rubbed his eyes.

At your service! Though I am not sure which service you are in . . .

The driver brother coughed loudly into his hand.

The guard leaned down until his head filled the space of the window. Saladin saw waves of the day's heat come off the head in a gaseous halo.

And you? Another brother rushing home to suck from maman's dried-up teat?

Yes!

Ali announced.

I am going to go home and suck the dried teat. It is the best, you must know.

The guards eyes hardened with suspicion, and Ali's manner fell even looser and he started to laugh into his hand as if a funny joke had just been told.

The guard straightened and stepped back from the car.

Okay, baba. Out. All of you.

Yes, of course, let me get my bag first. I cannot go anywhere without this bag. You will want to look in it I am sure . . .

Ali grabbed the leather satchel and began to open his door, and the driver brother jumped out and ran to push Ali back in and slam the door. He stood beside the guard and apologized in a grave, calm voice.

Please, agha, you must excuse him. You are completely right, of all the brothers he is the one who needs our maman's milk the most. Bechareh. He was born like that. We can't even take proper care of him. He sits in the mosque all day and keeps the hajii agha company. He's stuck with the mind of a schoolboy. Look, he carries that dirty satchel everywhere he goes. It's full of the same books he had in the first class! We have to take him home to Maman. Only she can care for him.

The guard looked at Ali and then at the driver. He looked at the bag on Ali's lap and then back at Ali, and his face pulled in and then down and his attitude deflated. He walked away from the car and the brother and waved his hand carelessly in the air.

Go. Boro. And take your idiot brother with you. Our new country has no place for fools. Trust we will not let him in again.

The driver brother jumped around the hood and into the driver's seat and started the car. The arm lifted and he drove cautiously past the kiosk and away from the checkpoint as Ali, like a child, pushed his head, and then shoulders and chest, out the window, and soon it seemed as if his whole body would fall out of the car and drag on the pavement.

Ali!

Saladin shouted.

The car had turned a corner and the driver brother picked up speed just as the passenger brother turned around in his seat and grabbed the waist of Ali's pants and pulled him back in. He grabbed the leather satchel from Ali's lap and smacked his face with a heavy, open hand. You thought you could stay? You thought you could make us stay? Get us in trouble?

The car moved fast now, faster than Saladin had ever felt a car move. Everything—the car, the violence, the drop of blood that fell from Ali's brow—was happening with quickness. Beneath them the wheels spun in rapid rotations, the pistons moved diligently in their shafts, and every second they were all pushed farther and farther from Iran. Locked in a speeding car filled with violence, Saladin tucked his hands between his thighs and looked down and wished for a smooth ride, a happy time, a brother who did not bleed.

The passenger brother shouted at Ali with a fury that turned his pale face red. Just wait until you get to Van. There is nothing there. We should just leave you here, throw you out to die on the side of this road!

Ali did not flinch. His posture slumped but his eyes stayed forward. Saladin had known his brother to fight, to always fight, but in this new land, his brother was limp. The passenger brother cursed a few more times and eventually turned, and everything, except for the sound of the speed, went quiet. Saladin looked out the window and felt his chest heave. He tried to keep the tears down, back behind his throat, in his stomach and gut, and focused his attention on what passed outside, a dry and empty landscape not one boulder different, not one shade changed, from the land they had left.

FAR ENOUGH

ONLY AFTER WE cross the border do the questions come.

Only if we were not caught or harassed or tortured on the spot or sent back in army camions do we let ourselves ask, How? For that is a question we save until it is done and we are on the other side, flooded by the first sweat of relief or torrent of tears or prayers to a God we promise to believe in until we die. Only after the crossing with our dreams and direction intact can the men and women of the Iranian exodus stand on the other side of an invisible line and point to a mountain or clump of rocks or expanse of dry fields and wonder:

How far now?

How is it that here, in this nothing, we are safer than in that nothing over there?

Where is the guarantee that we can make a home or a love or a life in this place?

At the first stop after the border we stand, by all means free, and look around to notice that not one thing keeps the long, dark shadows of home from creeping across this random, invisible border and strangling our still-shaking frames.

All right then. How far from here?

And because no one has an answer, the panic surges in those first kilometers as we find this other side is exactly the same as that from which we came. Stuck in this monotony of motion, the men and women of the migration look around again and ask, incredulous, If this earth and rock and sky have not at all changed, then what did?

We keep on. Drive more kilometers, walk more steps, take more buses into the new landscapes and think:

Maybe here? Maybe here it will be different. This might be far enough. When will I know how far is enough? How?

The roads are all made of the same asphalt, the buildings held up by the same mortar, and the air tastes no different in our open mouths. Even as the language changes and none of the words we know suffice to buy a newspaper or order a kebab or find the bathroom or embassy or way out, there is no relief, just the confused faces and useless silence. More kilometers, more movement, more languages and more borders, and soon we begin to fear that maybe all the distance in the world will not do.

Still, we keep going until the roads end in cities where we are reassured by the bustle of cars and countless residents who insist on living their lives as usual. We catch sight of the spires of mosques and hear the azan repeated, and it hits us like a punch and a kiss, as it is familiar but a reminder too of an old home that has pushed us out. And though we know we have moved far, we realize it may not be far enough and so we keep on.

It will spread.

We whisper to one another.

As long as there are believers, who is to say Khomeini's craze cannot be a craze here? Who can say Turkey is not next? Pakistan? Iraq? What if soon it will be a curse to be a Jew or Baha'i or Kurd everywhere? Where to go?

In truth we know it is not the believers, believers who have been our teachers and neighbors, bakers and dear friends, but the fervor that has just overtaken them. A fervor for change and pride and self-worth that makes it impossible for us to all live together, hold our varying beliefs alongside. We take stock of the first stops and move on like faulty pilgrims, away from belief into disbelief, persecuted for our love of another God and in search of some new and unknown home.

Around us scripts begin to change, the scales of music shift and the smells and textures of food open sensations in us we have never had. The earth sprouts dense forests of high trees and ends at unfathomable seas, but the sky stays the same and we move beneath it with the intuition of migrating birds and fish, forward to some sight unseen, to some farther point, and we do not falter, convinced, as pilgrims are convinced, that home will be found.

For each, the journey has its own end.

Some stop at the familiar faces of family who have gone before. Some stop at a job or a house. Some stop at the beauty and charm of a Rome or Paris or London they had only seen in films or magazines and let themselves believe the fantasy for a time. For others, it is land or money or fear that ends and they simply settle where they do and let exhaustion answer all their questions.

Here. Here is good. Why not? For now.

Most do not stop until everything the eye passes over and the nose smells and the heart feels is foreign, wholly unfamiliar, alien and so, possible. When little is recognizable, they wander about and keep an eye out for the ways they can enter, put down their bags, stay. For many the distance is far, and then just like that it is enough and they drop their shoulders, open their eyes to meet the eyes of the new people around them and take the reins of a life as they planned it. Here the men and women of the exodus unpack and light cigarettes or take apartments and finally walk the streets without luggage and nod their heads.

Yes.

Here.

Now.

And like that we give ourselves the permission to sit and sleep and stay.

SUNSETS

THE BOARDWALK IS busier now than when Saladin started his walk. He wants to push forward and find a stretch of tall buildings, some other face of Los Angeles, but the crowds are thick and he must stop and start with them as they are fascinated by dancers and magicians and men who twist balloons into small animals. He passes in front of a building boarded over with painted planks of woods that advertise unbelievable oddities. Outside it a man with a thick mustache stands behind a wooden block almost as high as his nose. Carefully he leans forward and makes a show of placing his tongue flat on the surface of the block, and then another show of centering a nail on top of his extended tongue, and yet another show of presenting a hammer and slamming three times into the nail, the flesh of the tongue, the block of wood. There are applause and bows but no blood. He wears a green turban like a Hindu and no shirt. After the tongue he puts small nails through the septum of his nose and then the ears and finally the thin webbing between the fingers of the hand. Pierced, he stands and rotates for all to see. Some take pictures, a few whisper to one another and fewer clap. The rest of the boardwalk passes by until Saladin is the last one standing. The man gestures him to a nearby cage, where a woman sits in a fitted leopard-print leotard, reading a magazine and twirling a dirty tail.

Saladin cannot take her as cartoon or real so he understands her as a local species somewhere in between. He turns away from the ticket booth and walks to the shore. A dull pull of hunger make his gut hot, and he stands against the railing to take in the cool wind of the sea. A few feet away two young girls stand beside bicycles. One smokes a cigarette and stares out at the water. The other combs her almost yellow hair with a black plastic comb. Saladin sees the low-cut blouses, shoes without socks, lips and eyes with no traces of time or worry around the edges, and steps to the girls, midday wind off the sea like a goading hand at his back.

Hello. Please. What is time?

The smoking girl squints at him, checks her watch and then speaks.

Twelve oh six.

Hello.

As he has seen the men in the motorcycle movies do, Saladin stands with both of his hands in his back pockets and pushes his chest out to look cool, comfortable and calm. He repeats, Hello.

The face of the girl with the comb darkens and the smoking girl laughs.

Come on. Be nice. He's cute.

The smoking one asks.

Well, hello yourself. What's your name?

Saladin smiles at the one question he recognizes and answers too quickly.

My name is Saladin.

And he wants to go on to explain, to tell her it is the hero's name, after Saladin of the Ayyubids. Great Kurdish crusader, foe to Richard the Lionheart himself, father to orphans and protector of widows. The name of a conqueror whose courage is still spoken of in all the mountain towns of the Zagros. Warrior who defeated the Christian troops in Tikrit, Basra, at the golden dome in Jerusalem. He says nothing and instead straightens his back and tries to transmute these and other integrities with his posture, his eyes and his smile. He tries again.

I like you dress. Very beautiful.

The girls look down at their shorts and blouses and sandals, and the laughing one laughs and the one with yellow hair says nothing. They roll their bikes away from him into the crowd, and Saladin has no more desire for this day. His appetite is gone and all he craves is to be inside, in a dark room with no windows on this world. He goes to the ticket booth where the woman in the cat costume still twirls her long, soft tail.

How much? Inside?

He points to the boarded up building.

The woman drops her tail.

A dollar.

The woman does not look up and repeats herself. Saladin knows she has just spoken a price he cannot pay, but he stands there until she looks up at him again.

Fine. Go ahead. It's too early anyway. You won't see anything.

Saladin walks through the black wooden doors into a dark hall, where he makes his way from one elaborately painted image to the next, feats and scenarios he cannot believe though they are advertised as right there, behind the door exactly as painted: fantastic and live with breath.

On the first door is an image of a blond woman with her legs behind her head, thighs open to the world. He pushes at the door to find a young girl with long, straight, black hair and blue paint on her fingers and toes. Her limbs are thick and her eyes are dull, and after a few seconds she sticks her tongue out at Saladin, a gesture both childish and serpentine. On the next door the painting shows a muscular man swallowing a knife. The man who answers Saladin's knocks is fat and wears thin pajamas. He keeps one hand on his crotch and the other on a cigarette.

What?

One door has the painted image of a pale-skinned woman. Her breasts are full and her smile allures, but for the tremendous beard that grows around and under it. Saladin pushes open the door and knows no matter what is behind it, he will enter, he will sit and rest in a cool room.

A black woman sits in front of the small television screen. She does not look at Saladin but speaks loudly in his direction.

Honey, please! Close that door. Don't let all that heat in.

And it is welcome enough. She is not at all the woman advertised on the door but her room is as dark and cold as he wants it to be, and as Saladin takes a few steps in, she asks.

You going to sit?

And points to an empty place next to her on the couch. She

takes up long silver needles and clinks them together to weave one thread of yarn into a long piece of sweater or shawl. Saladin does not have the language to explain that the women of the mountain town did the same thing, but with wooden needles, that everything that has kept him warm has been made this way. He takes the seat beside her and watches the television, a show of policemen on an island that is regularly interrupted by breaks in which men and women and children brush their teeth, drive cars, clean kitchens and eat whipped cream. In truth he is more interested in the old woman. He has never seen skin so brown, so old. Her face is slack, and most of the visible wrinkles are on her hands. The hair on her head is short and wiry and white, and her eyes reflect the television in a blurred glow. The show ends and she leans forward and shuts off the machine with a loud grunt.

She turns to Saladin.

Hrmph. You look just about as lost as you can be.

If he tried, he might be able to understand the words she sings slowly out of her mouth, but he is distracted by the hairs that sprout from the area where her chin meets her neck. The beard is unconvincing, almost an accident on this woman who is, in all other ways, a woman, with long breasts and small shoulders and thin, nimble fingers.

I knew you were coming. Yes. They all come to me. Some at the beginning. Some later.

The voice is easy to listen to, melodic and soft like an owl's call or a lullaby. Her eyes focus on him and Saladin notices they are not green or blue or black but almost no color at all, lighter than blue, dirtier than white. He tries to match their gauzy, intent stare.

Your mama. She is dead. Is that right? Is your mother dead?

Saladin recognizes the word and looks to the old woman for more, but there is no more. *Morde*, he thinks. He wants to explain, I am here because of my mother. This was a dream for her. For me. But she is dead. Since I was eleven. I came in her place. She would be very proud of me. In America.

The old woman nods as if she has heard all the thoughts that crossed his mind, and Saladin feels comfort from this old mother who mentions his mother. They sit together in an easy silence for some time.

Yes. That's what I thought. Mama is always the first home . . . but you'll find your way. You won't be lost forever.

A small smile dances at the edge of her lips and then dissolves, and another face takes the place of the face she wore just a second ago. Her eyes close and her lower lip drops open.

You had a brother too. You had a brother once. Al? Albert? Alley? Ali. Ali.

The sound of the name spoken out loud splinters in Saladin's gut, and he is quick off the couch and quick out the house of false diversions and on the boardwalk before the old woman has opened her eyes. The sun is a half circle now, partly hidden by the flat line of the sea, and he looks for a place to take a shit, a place to relieve himself of the nerves that have exploded inside him, but the boardwalk is full of people stopped to watch the sunset. He ignores the oohs and ahhs and steps on their shadows and runs back to the beach where he slept, back to the only place he knows. In running, the urge to shit disappears and he searches the sand to find the divot his body made just last night. Every inch of the beach is the same, indistinguishable. Everywhere a shivering child runs out of the sea, and everywhere a mother waits, towel spread wide. He cannot stand these and other sights and moves on and searches for some far beacon.

Ahead, a pier juts far into the ocean, and Saladin goes toward it for no reason other than it is a landmark his eyes can focus on. When he gets to the long structure, he sees a place, just beneath, where the wooden planks of the pier meet the planks of the boardwalk. It is low and covered and broad, a space for him to tuck himself, to hide. The sand is cold and smells of urine, but he spreads out his body anyway, lies flat on his back and waits for his breath to slow, for night to come, for sleep. As on the night before, memories come instead of sleep, and he thinks of the last time he stretched out on a beach and waited to disappear.

The smugglers left the brothers at the lip of an enormous lake.

Go. Get out. Walk around like the idiots you are. It will be only a matter of hours before the border police find you and send you back.

They offered no instructions or farewells, and the car was gone before either Saladin or Ali had taken his first step.

The afternoon was warm and sunny. The brothers walked on a pebbly beach that sank beneath their feet and tried their best to avoid the families and groups gathered to picnic at sunset. The smell of food plagued them both, but neither brother mentioned it. Saladin let his mouth water and Ali walked slowly past the giant copper pots of fragrant stew. They had no money and no conversations about money and kept on as if they had no need.

Farther down the beach they passed a family speaking Farsi. A mother and grandmother, father and three sons. They had with them sandwiches of bologna and potato salads, thermoses of tea and small almond desserts. Saladin could not stop himself, not with shame or manners, and he leaned down.

Excuse me, agha. I beg your pardon, we heard your Farsi and . . .

The father looked once at Saladin and once at Ali. He put a hand up to silence Saladin.

Are you leaving Iran? Do you have to leave Iran too?

Saladin did not answer. The man said a few words to his wife, and she looked at him helplessly before handing over a wrapped sandwich and a tin of cookies.

Many apologies. It is all we have. Like you, we have come a long way, like you we have a long way to go. Inshallah, we will all see each other in a better place. Inshallah.

The man did not smile. He did nothing more than pass the two items, but Saladin felt as if they had just met a martyr. He thanked him profusely and waited for Ali to say something, but his brother stared out over the water and made no remarks. They walked away until they were far from the families and the picnics and alone on a narrow stretch of beach. Ali sat in front of a smooth boulder and Saladin sat a few feet away, and quietly they ate. The sun dropped, and two birds of a sort Saladin had never seen, long legged and white, flew close to the surface of the lake.

See, Ali. Many people are going.

Ali said nothing. He picked up handfuls of pebbles and tossed them into the lake.

Many are going. It is not just us.

Ali's mood hardened. Every handful of pebbles grew heavier, fell farther from where they sat.

Many are cowards. Just like us.

But they are going. They have to go too.

Where are they going? Where? You don't even know where we are now. We have crossed the border, it will only be harder to get back.

Saladin kept his eyes on the birds, the pale mark they made on the sky. What birds were they? What birds were there in the world?

His brother went on.

You move like a man made of dreams, Saladin jaan. I blame Maman, she took you to that stupid cinema, told you, *Of course, jaan am, you can go to Amreeka.* And now look at you, look at me. Two brothers on the way to nowhere. We belong to that town, to our sisters, to the life there. Only the weak leave at the first sign of danger. The strong stay, with their people. Their homes.

Behind them the old town of Van pressed its ancient buildings up against the sky, and Saladin saw rooftops spiked with antennae, the glass of their windows murky and dull. There were balconies and a few cars, but no promenades filled with pretty girls and no cinema marquees. It was a town no better than the mountain town. The sun dropped and a few women started to set up their wares, copper pots, knitted shawls, jars of pickled radishes, onions and beets, for the night sale. Saladin knew the taste of the radishes, the feel of the shawls, and his stomach churned with the idea of going back, of a life of knowing things he had always known, a life in which he had caused death.

Ali. We have killed. We might have killed men.

His brother skipped a stone forcefully across the water.

You don't know what happened to the guards you shot. They all fell. The men I shot, the ones I hit, might not have been dead yet. Maybe I have killed men who might have lived. Maybe you have killed men in the new army.

Ali found a large rock and threw it in. It hit and sank with a loud splash. Across the lake the white birds jumped up and flew. He lay back on the sand with one hand behind his head and one hand on his stomach, his face drained of energy, his breaths in and out of his ribs in slow, steady pulses. He closed his eyes.

I am tired, now. Let's sleep. It is warm here, no one will bother us on this beach. Tomorrow we will know.

Saladin fell back, and pebbles printed themselves into his shirt and then his skin. He took in the soft blue of the sky as it turned gray and then navy and finally all black like the edits of black between scenes in films, the moment of total dark that allows for change.

Under the pier Saladin lets the memories come and go. They were tired as he is tired now. They were upset, as he is upset now. And that day, just as this day now, was over and there was little to do in the night but sleep. At the end of the beach the ocean is big with waves and white wash, and heavy waters slam into the pillars of the pier. Saladin closes his eyes tight and feels the vibration of the wood through his bones and muscles, and after a time the heavy rhythm calms him and he is gone, finished with his first American day and off to a sleep that is neither here nor there.

LEFT BEHIND

THERE ARE THOSE of us who cannot leave.

You go. Take your fear and nerves and your *What if?* And *If then?* And *Ay, Khoda*s. Take with you all the selfish and small-minded thoughts but do not try to take us. We, the brothers and fathers and sisters and cousins and neighbors and friends, will stay here, in our apartments and houses, in our gardens and among our dead. This revolution does not bother us. Life is life.

But you have no imagination! you shout.

For what! we ask. For the stories and lies you tempt us with?

It will be just like Tehran or Esfahan, lovelier than Shiraz, you say. It will be better, less dangerous, more free.

Free? We tilt our stubborn heads and ask, What is free? You will have nowhere to point and say, There, there is where I; or, Here, at this corner is where I; or, That is my primary school and this is where my baba works, look, there is my uncle right now, under the hood of that car. He loves that car. All the men in this village have my surname. You get angry when we say this and shout at us, Use your imagination!

Pfff. For what?

Later we will let you know, in phone calls or letters, that we were right.

We will call and say, Yes, things are hard, yes, and the world is upside down here, but we were right to stay. Just last night for example we simply tucked ourselves into the comfortable known beds, and when the noise of the garbageman tossing over an empty can or a sharp dream of you in peril woke us up in the middle of the night, everything was there. The old pillowcase, the photographs of you as a baby, the guitar we shared, the painting our old, dead uncle made, the light of the bright streetlamp outside, made a force of familiarity to guide our minds, our unsettled souls, most directly and easily back to sleep, back home. Come on now, what more do we need before we die? That is enough.

We will pray for you, for your journey, for your crossing. Worry not, we have enough imagination for that.

And, yes, the days will come when our hands will itch from want. Want for the touch of our brother's rough hand, our daughter's supple shoulders, and our beloved's warm cheek. We busy our hands with chores, feel over the objects we have known all life long—the calcium-stained faucet, the doorknob to the hyatt, the bottom button of the wool sweater whose color refuses to change—and think of you and all the generations you have taken with you, away, all of you gone now on journeys complete with small paradises and many little hells.

Days will come when our feet itch from the want of a walk with you down the labyrinths of the bazaar where we busy ourselves with errands of the outside world and keep our heads down as we trace yesterday's steps to the baker, the teahouse, the woman with the best paneer, and try to forget you in the pleasures of the daily back and forth.

Days pass as they will. After the every-night noise of the television news and radio news that mention nothing of your safe arrival, your quick death, your long purgatory in some strange city where no one is kind, we sit in silence. The silence stays. It fills the space between the waves of longing and our attempts at joy and celebration. Such is life. We will stay and keep this Iran. Let the others go and start a new life elsewhere . . .

Maybe you are still traveling when Iraq invades the western border? It is September 1980. The leaves on the trees of our street have just begun to turn, and within months we sit surrounded by barren winter branches and listen to the silence between bombs and think of you, of ourselves, of this life and other things. We wash clean our hands and feet and ears and nostrils and we pray. We touch the things you have touched—the stuffed toy, the American rock record, the key to the yard—and we wonder, Are we, here on the verge of death, more alive than you? For we are here, living, while you have gone and that seems now like a kind of death? That you can no longer touch the things you touched, that your marks are slowly being rubbed off all that was once familiar, is a disappearing that is no different from death.

We pray for you. Pray and wait, for though we are stuck here, in this back land with the falling bombs and food lines and masked ceremonies of devotion, there will come a time when our spirits will travel to meet you in some place in the between, some place at the end of days.

In the months after you leave, we are forced to imagine you. How can we not? There is so much empty time in the first weeks there. Time we used to fill with drawn-out, pointless arguments over tea and cigarettes in the kitchen, protracted, roundabout walks that took us to your mother's house or my uncle's house, where we sat and waited for the evening to be over. With the beloved, the grandfather, the brother, the cherished daughter, life takes its time. Everything is faster when you are alone.

So we fill the time with thoughts of you and imagine how it is where you are. Around us everything is the same, and some things are worse. The stores offer less variety. There is talk of war though no one wants to hear it. The cinemas are shut down and the universities have refused students for more than a month now. Even the most regular things have been given new names. Shah's Square is now Azadi Square, my brother insists we call him by his full name, Hossein Abdullah, for the sake of propriety before God. To anger him I just call him boy. In this unremarkable sadness we think of you and know nothing around you is the same.

Do you like what you see? What does the food taste like? Are the people kind? Is the sun the same color, the moon just as meaningful as it is here? Do you stop under the new sky to miss us?

It is not uncommon to slip up, imagine ourselves alongside you in the new lands, eating the strange foods, waiting for transport, nervously clutching our passports and visas and important documents, taking the bus, boat, train. We remember the trips we have taken together in the past, as far as the Caspian Sea, as close as the bakery down the street, and this brings to mind the trips we had planned: the anticipation of dinners in Paris, nights of dancing at Roman discotheques, the photos we would take beside the Statue of Liberty's stiff flame. We imagine you might do these things without us, and here our imaginings end. It is too exhausting to think of you enjoying our plans; to think of you alone enjoying anything at all is, at times, too difficult to bear.

We start to fill our time with other things, none of them as beloved as you, dear, but we make them important. School, the new job, our sick parents—all become obsessions and distractions. As you gain distance in the world, distance from us, we train ourselves to think of you less. Only on occasion—of your birthday, the day we run into your mother or brother in the market, the anniversary of the day you left—do the imaginings come again strong and fierce and beyond our control and we wonder if you imagine us still.

Do you imagine us? In the boredom of long bus rides, in the hustle and pleading of embassy waiting rooms, when you are alone in some dark without sleep? We like to imagine you think of us then, but it does not escape us that you might also think of us when another eye catches your eye, when some flesh lust draws your attention or when a proposition is made by glance or saunter or laugh. We like to think that you think of us then, remember us, love us even more deeply, from afar.

How do you reach the ones who have gone? Can it be enough to sit and concentrate on their names? Their faces? The habits of their hands? Can you close your eyes and wish for them to hear the thoughts in your head, the cravings in your soul? After a time we recognize it is not in our control. The old, adamant mothers and aged fathers pray to reach you. They call up to God one or two or five times a day for your health, your safe journey and successful arrival as you slip between worlds. They pray to reach you as you travel through that middle place where only faith can go.

Let the old pray. We will pass the time with our visions of you eating ice cream in Spain, playing volleyball on a beach in Los Angeles, wearing a cowboy hat in Texas, smiling into an invisible camera, waving and planning our inevitable reunion. And when we no longer have the energy to conjure the image of you loving us from afar, missing us, wishing we were there, we imagine the days we had, the afternoons of slippery games in the shallow rivers, the summer nights asleep under the stars, the shape of your face in the mirror, until even those memories grow into fictions, stories from a past for which we will soon no longer have proof.

HEROES

A TRUCK DRIVER from Taquboustan found them playing soccer with a pinecone. Saladin and Ali shouted back and forth in a mixture of languages, and the truck driver stopped and listened.

Brothers?

He asked in Kurdish.

They stopped their game and said nothing.

If you are here.

He pointed at the lake.

It must mean that you cannot be there.

He pointed east, back to Iran. His Kurdish was odd, chopped off at the edges.

Come. I am going west, to Ankara and then Istanbul. I will give you a ride.

And just as Ali opened his mouth to resist, to say they had not yet made up their minds and Van might be far enough, but thank you, the driver held up the palm of his hand.

Please. I know what it is like to be a Kurd where Kurds are despised. You should go. Van is not safe.

They drove for three days and stopped four times for petrol and twice for the driver to sleep fitfully in the back of the cab. They spoke little and listened to the strange music that came from the endless cassette tapes he kept under his seat. They arrived in Istanbul at night, and the driver stopped the truck in front of an enormous concrete building without windows.

The foreman is a friend, a Kurd as well. He knows me. Tell him I sent you and he will give you work, and food. The city is big enough. You will be left alone. Khodafez.

The foreman was a tall, bald man with ink stained deep into his fingernails. In a mix of Kurdish and Turkish he explained the work: a printing press, for a daily newspaper, not left, not right, something in the middle . . . the machines are old and moody and need attention. He offered to pay them time and a half. You know, for night hours. And at the end of their first day his wife had set up a meal of okra stew, bread and rice on a small plastic table in the courtyard behind the press. When they left, it was dawn and they found themselves in a huge city of tiered fountains and water taxis, seas that glistened gold and skies that spread above them in bright oranges and pinks.

During their first week in Istanbul the brothers could take no wrong steps. They moved across high and low bridges, off and on water buses and down busy boulevards where bodies bumped into them without apology. They explored hilly neighborhood streets lined with five- and six-story apartment buildings where children and laundry and cats held on to railings and defied all gravity. Whenever he could, Saladin let himself go blind with the constant lights of cars and signs and storefronts, deaf from the shouts and blares of every hidden radio and television and record player. And in that first week the brothers did not close their jaws or steel themselves to the laughter of passing girls.

They arrived at the printing press each evening at ten and left each morning at six with money carefully folded in their pockets and stomachs full of the same okra stew. They walked through the waking city until they found a clean and grassy park where they slept with newspaper pillows and newspaper shades and woke rested and warm. In the afternoons they walked down the waterfront promenades and sampled the sweet ice cream and candies.

One afternoon they came across a group of men playing a fast and youthful game of soccer in a flat, mostly green park. They stood at the edges long enough for someone to call out to them in Turkish, and when it happened, the brothers looked at each other and jogged to join in. Ali went to the opposite end of the pitch, and Saladin shouted, *Careful with your fancy tricks!* And just as in the mountain town he did his best to guard his brother but could not keep up as Ali took passes that came from nowhere and escaped with the ball as if it belonged only to him and not to the team or the game. No matter how Saladin tried to keep Ali in the corner of his eye, he was always gone and down the field, and for every one of his three goals Saladin was forced to laugh and curse and laugh again as the other team clapped his brother's shoulder and shook his brother's hand.

★ ★ ★

That night they ate dinner at a sidewalk café on a busy commercial street. The waiter served them without taking their order, and small dishes of fried and cured foods came out one after another. When two green bottles of beer were placed before them, the brothers did not resist, and Saladin raised his as he had seen done in movies and Ali joined, and in the sudden grip of pleasure that comes with doing anything for the first time, Saladin toasted.

To America!

He put his bottle down without drinking. Embarrassment filled his face and he stared away from the table to hide it. What was wrong with him? Why did some part of his heart, his head, his body, insist on America? Why wasn't this enough? There were lights, and noise, they were far. Ali was not happy but he was not upset or mean. Saladin looked out at the street. It was full of walkers and shoppers and other eaters and drinkers spilled out onto the sidewalk. There were women in stylish sunglasses and high-heel shoes like stilts and men with briefcases and mustaches and thin jackets. The storefronts were filled with same-faced mannequins in blond wigs and light dresses, and every inch of wall that was not glass was covered with posters advertising films he had never heard of, from Italy, France, Hollywood. He knew that all he saw around him, the expertise and fashion and attitude, came from someplace else, from America, and Saladin wanted not this simulacrum or reproduction but the origin, the actual thing, the first place. From beyond the din of the street the sound of a muezzin blared with the high, nasal voice of a mullah that wove itself into all the other noises until it was indistinguishable, both ever present and disappeared. Ali smiled and took a sip of beer. He grimaced briefly, then smiled. He began to eat heartily.

An amazing city, no, Saladin jaan? Even if Maman had told us about it, read about it in one of her books, I would not have believed her. So much water! Can you believe it? The city just ends in the water, to the west and south. Unless you are a fish, there is no place to go.

Ali smacked happily on the bones of some small creature.

But, I must thank you.

For what?

You knew it. I don't know how, but you were right. No one recognizes us. The city is big. There is work, it is easy to live day to day, and when the time comes, simple to go back. We can go the way we came. Trucks to Ankara, Van, then over the mountains, then home. This is the right place for us. For now. You were right to keep walking, to bring us to this city where we are safe. I am grateful.

Saladin had no energy to argue. Ali shook the empty beer bottle in the air until the waiter noticed. When another beer appeared, Ali took another sip and, in a voice reserved for elders, for the old Kurds they were told to respect without knowing why, announced, bottle in the air.

To our hero.

Saladin did not match the gesture. That word had only come from his brother a few times, and only when he talked of the famous men of the mountain, dead men who gave their lives to keep the town and the Kurds in it. By his brother's definition Saladin was no hero. He had fled, like a coward, and now he wanted to follow an uncertain dream, for fear of the nightmare just behind. It was his brother who was brave, the hero, as they knew the word. A long time passed and Saladin could not meet his brother's eye.

Saladin looked at his lap and then to the street where a trio of girls giggled and the traffic of a few cars stopped. It was a city, yes, bigger than the mountain town, fuller with the traffic of cars, and, yes, the people had fashionable clothes and attitudes but everything else about them was similar—hair and eyes and skin—to that of the people Saladin had known his whole life. He imagined explaining Istanbul to his mother, the ways in which it was different, the ways in which it was the same. Even in the imaginary conversation he felt her disappointment, heard her chide, *But you have gone so far. You are so much closer! If only you went a bit more, it would be just as we imagined. Amreeka. California* . . . Saladin watched his brother eat and drink like a happy traveler, a man who enjoys everything of the new worlds because his heart is always at home, warm and tucked away like some white ember. A feeling came upon Saladin and he sensed that the shape of his life, as he planned it, was changing. What he long imagined to be a straight line, a mark, arrow-led, dream-led, from the mountain town to Los Angeles, California, America, could also take the form of a circle, a round and closed loop, here and back. The trio of girls brought their laughter closer and lit cigarettes they pulled at through thick, colored lips. Saladin stood and the girls smiled.

Our hero.

His brother repeated in Kurdish, and Saladin pulled a few bills from his pocket.

Work is not for a few hours yet, baba. And these girls. We should invite them for a beer. Here . . . I have a few lira too . . .

Let's go to work. I want to go now. Please, Ali. Let's go.

Ali smiled at the girls and left a small mass of bills and change on the table and ran to catch up to Saladin.

Okay. Okay. You never worked so hard in Kermanshah.

His brother punched Saladin's shoulder lightly.

Who knows? Maybe travel is good for you.

There was some relief in work. They worked apart, and the presses made enough noise that Saladin could not hear Ali's chipper whistle. They kept to their own corners, and Saladin let his thoughts whir to the speed of the oily machines until he was flooded in questions and lost to wonderings: Why is my brother so glad? Is this the end? Where is the end? How do you stop? When do you stop? Why? How do brothers leave a city of water if they cannot, like fish or whales, swim?

Except for the mess, the work that night was no different from all the nights before. How many nights had it been since they arrived? Six? Seven? More? What was happening to time? Each day the paper printed a date on the top right corner, and every day Saladin ignored it. He did not know how long it had been since they had left, or even how long it was to where they were going, and he realized that all the days fell, one after the next like rain or snow, irrespective of what came before or after. These thoughts of time, its loss and gain, the knowing that the days before no longer belonged and the days to come were unknown and blank, confused Saladin to the point of panic.

The morning's headline was large and followed by a half-page photograph. The extra ink for the font and photo slowed the machines with wet-balled jams that made a mess of his hands and arms, but Saladin paid little attention and worked steadily at clearing the rollers and cogs as they became stuck, his mind and mouth occupied with arrangements, arguments and pleas. *Ali, we must leave tomorrow because . . . Ali, we must get out of Istanbul or else . . . Ali, we cannot stay, they will find us here . . . I don't know how, but the mullahs will . . .* Various and frantic, none of them felt convincing enough, and his steps dragged from paper jam to paper jam as he felt his own best efforts wane. The city had swallowed them and they were safe. When the machines came to a sharp halt and a thousand fans and belts and gaskets went silent, Saladin heard the sound of his own unconvincing voice, begging, out loud, *But, Ali . . . we must.*

The foreman shouted for everyone to wait. Saladin looked for somewhere to sit that wouldn't mark his only pair of pants. At his feet the concrete was splashed with twenty years of ink, and the pages of the next day's paper were already making a messy second layer. He stood and stared at his feet and, below them, the day's headline and front-page photo.

As it was in life, it was in the photograph. A firing squad. A green valley. A line of crouching, faceless executioners with rifles for arms and bullets for selves. Eleven revolutionary guards, eleven men shot, three fallen, seven falling and one still upright, his bandaged hand over his heart, his face calm the instant before death. Even in black and white, the valley was clearly wet from a recent rain. A ring of mountains circled all the distances of the photo, and at the far end of the firing squad a tall, satisfied mullah stood beside a captain with a clumped and spotty face, the ink blurred in the small space where his features should have been. In the foreground of the photo stood the heads and shoulders and silhouettes of two boys, men maybe, brothers even, so similar were they in their height and shape and disbelief.

* * *

Waves slam into the pier and Saladin jolts from sleep and hits his head on the low, wooden beams of the pier. It is day again. Another day, the second in America, and where he wants to celebrate or excite, but there is a pain in his head and a deep ache of hunger in the center of him. Did he dream it? What did he dream? Ali drowning in the Bosporus, just out of Saladin's reach. Saladin shouting to his brother, *Swim. Swim. You can swim!* His brother flapping in the water like a bird. The small tugboat floating by and the two Turkish men with hooks for hands picking Ali out from the water, taking him to a safety Saladin cannot see. Terror in the details. Saladin's hoarse shouts, the hooked hands, his brother's wet back, safe on the boat, moving away.

Saladin slides his body sideways until it is out from underneath the wood shelter of the pier and extends now to the pale yellow light of early morning. The beach is misty and emptier than when he fell asleep, but otherwise just as he left it yesterday: the enormous sea, flat and without mark, the boardwalk and the scattered trash. He cracks his neck and shakes out his clothes and walks away from the ocean and the sand, through the tiny streets of Venice's neighborhoods and the even tinier alleys between houses, and though he is nowhere and his whole life this morning is without certainty or plan, Saladin walks confident and tall, sure these streets will lead to bigger streets, to a center of the Los Angeles where all life meets.

WHAT DOES AND DOES NOT FOLLOW

THIS IS WHAT does not follow us when we go.

Our grandmother's tea set, the eight gilded glasses and their saucers, antiques by now. Sentimental, we know, but no other glasses will sound the same when clinked together, no other saucers held the hot tea my grandfather would pour into a pool and blow on until just cool enough.

The favorite towel does not come after us. Where did it come from anyway? We can't remember, but it was always there, waiting for us to come out of the bath. Soft enough to absorb water, thin enough that we could still feel our muscles and bones beneath. Who would have thought a towel could be kind, but it was, in its own way.

The Chinese lamp does not follow, the one our uncle made when he began his fascination with simple electrical wiring.

Look!

He would call from the basement.

I've wired this cheap, imported vase and now it is a lamp!

And though we wanted to make fun of him, he was right, it was an elegant object as long as you didn't look inside . . . the stone chessboard; the rosewood-and-pearl backgammon table; the smooth pieces; the lucky dice. We should have brought the lucky dice. The smell of camphor in our closets; the green-glass ashtray from the hyatt; the neighbor every afternoon who screams at her devilish son, his cries, their reconciliation, the sound of candy as it is unwrapped. The favorite cream puffs from sweetshops. The hajii agha who cleans the steps that lead up to the mosque, the shuffle of his slippers and his wet snorts.

The walk to the bakery does not follow us. How can it? With that lovely first corner in the shade, its second corner in the early sun, then the long stretch under the patched shadow of the Italian pines that hold the smell of warm yeast in their high, narrow boughs; the smell of hunger and its near-immediate end.

Though we may want otherwise, none of this comes with us when we go.

What follows us most ardently, in dogged pursuit like a neglected neighbor or a new ghost, is news of home. No matter how far we have gone, the distance between here and there irrelevant, the news—from newspapers at kiosks, the broadcasts on television sets at the back of restaurants, announcements on taxi radios—greets us when we arrive and helps send us further on our way.

It is there when we are looking and there when we are not. Dispatches, reports, official accounts, unofficial accounts, imagined and recounted accounts. As we said, in pursuit. Our dogged new friend.

We who left in '76, '77, '78, soothsayers every last one of us, heard the first reports of nationwide demonstrations; every city rallied to protest the Shah, the cruelty of SAVAK, the joblessness, poverty, the mysterious incarcerations and disappearances. February 1977 there were riots in every square, the public in public calling for better conditions, for a revision of their lives. And these were followed with brutal backlashes; the many dead (the actual number never exactly clear, never counted exactly) and the deaths demanded public rituals of mourning that spawned more riots, more deaths, more rituals and on and on; a cycle in spin, of its own energy, without end. We listened closely and watched carefully to know the exact details of the countrymen's dissatisfaction, sorrow and desperation and to know if it matched ours, and, yes, there were a few parallels, if not more.

We who leave early catch first sight and sound of this Ayatollah when he is still exiled in France. We listen to him speak gravely, incessantly, on behalf of all those oppressed by the regime of the Shah and demand that Iran be returned to the Iranians, to us. We wonder, who is this man? With a voice like a dear old father, its timbre soothing and soft, he calls for an end of exploitation of Iran by the British, the Americans, the rest; calls for a country built on itself, responsible and available to itself; calls for an Islamic state similar to the Islamic empires of ancient times; and promises what only a father can: to bring the people of this noble country *integrity, justice and a spiritual righteousness that can only come from God*. He gives a few television interviews and is always photographed among an entourage of journalists and mullahs, turbans and tape recorders in his face. And his face. We who leave early look carefully at that face, the heavy brow, the creased skin, the visage of a man complete and relaxed and not at all moved by the words that stream angry and quiet from his thin lips. What demons live in that turban, we wonder? What demons will be born from it? If we left in 1976, 1977, 1978, we listen, we know, we turn away, turn off and start moving.

Those of us who left in the early months of 1979 must have thought there was still a chance the country could be saved from chaos. But after the Black Friday Massacre in Shah Square, only the most naive among us could feign shock that the number of dead would be unknown, the arrests, countless. If there still remained a question in our heads—*Who knows what is going to happen?*—then the Cinema Rex fire answered it and we sat shocked before televisions and radios to hear that the entire cinema had burned to the ground with not one survivor among the four hundred in the audience. No one was alive to testify that masked men set the projector room on fire, escaped the building, barred the doors with long planks of wood, and did not let one soul out as they burned and pushed and burned. The building was lit for eighteen hours, and the spirits of the dead took their time floating up into the sky from which they followed the ball of blame as it was tossed from the Shah's insidious SAVAK to Khomeini's zealous supporters and back. No one claimed the crime. For many of us that was enough. When an evening out with your husband or mother or best friend is the death of you, when an afternoon at the cinema can kill, why stay? For what?

Still some of us, wishful, devoted, reluctant, remained to see the flames die down and the story play out. If we were there when the Shah turned his back to the cameras and boarded the plane, some thought, *Now. It is time.* Just as so many others who stayed, our brothers, sisters, cousins and friends, thought, *Thank God. Now, for Iran, it is time.*

Things changed quickly, and one minute we understood what had happened—a revolution to depose an unworthy shah, the possibility of a better future—and the next minute an Islamic state and mass arrests. Stalwarts among us, shortsighted optimists, needed the inspiration of an angry knock on the door, a rude search of our houses by some nameless komiteh guards, our telephones tapped or a few nights in jail.

Have you seen Agha X? It is known he lodged with you for a night. It would do well for you to admit this, to tell us where he has gone.

For some of us it took blood, ours, or that of our loved ones, spilled on the marble floors of our foyers and kitchens. For the most romantic it took a death in our homes or close to our hearts before we packed and fled.

Regardless. The news followed behind, biting at our heels. At the airport, train and bus stations, at the market, the embassy, in taxis and cinemas, on the street and in warm kitchens that didn't belong to us, the news was always there, nibbling.

Then came the photographs of April 17, 1979. An open massacre. Khomeini's first determined act is an offensive against the Kurds of the northwest. Eleven men put on trial, eleven verdicts of guilt, ranging from crimes against the new state, illegal loyalty to the Kurdish Democratic Party and on and on. The trial lasts twelve minutes and they are sentenced to immediate execution—the machinery of justice moves brusquely and by dinner everyone is dead. The photographer flees and the photos are broadcast all over the world. *Khomeini kills innocent Kurds! A massacre in the mountains!* Underneath the headlines is where we found him, the man to haunt us, to put air in our lungs and hurry our steps: the last man standing, hand on his heart, face calm, his executioner slow to fire. In the photographs we saw what the blindfolded eyes could not, and some of us stared. Some of us looked away. All of us kept going.

August 29, 1979: sweeping limitations on the press and all non-Islamic political organizations including the National Democratic Party, the Fedaiyan, the Tudeh.

November 1979: the American embassy in Tehran is overrun by armed students demanding the Shah be returned from the United States to Iran to stand trial. Hostages are taken, kept in poor conditions for 444 days, until liberated by the new president-elect, Ronald Reagan, a man recognized by the young Iranian hostage takers and American hostages alike as a famous actor.

Remember? The movie with the monkey? Bedtime for Bonzo*?* . . .

April 1980: the Islamic Cultural Revolution is instituted nationwide. *What does this mean?* we wondered. Those we left behind explained that the universities had been shut down and all curriculums revised. Courses in Western literature were canceled, history classes amended, Koranic studies made mandatory for all students, and men and women forced into separate classrooms, all women made to sit at the back of the bus. Sharia law was instated nationwide.

What?

We asked.

That ancient thing where every woman has to wear a veil and every thief has his hand severed?

We laughed nervously in the silence after their response.

If we had left by September 1980, the last of the news came chasing after us, tearing at the flesh of our ankles and heels and soft hearts. September 18, Iraqi army battalions invade the western border with Iran. Khomeini calls all boys of a certain age to the front, to their duty for the country and God. Just like that, the country is, for no reason, at war. We stopped to hear this last of all news, to let the bile of terror rise in our throats until we could no longer breathe. When the air came back to us, we turned off radios and televisions, folded newspapers and hung up telephones. We cried at bus stops, in the bathrooms of new jobs, in the dark of the cinema, in the park. We kissed the heads of our carefree children and took them out for ice cream, and still, even after we unplugged the machines, changed the subscriptions, kept the phones quiet, the broadcasts pursued us into our new homes, beds, nightmares and daydreams until the low crackle and constant buzz was with us everywhere, all the time, dogged, snapping, nipping, biting, devouring; as we rushed to catch the merry bells of the afternoon ice cream truck and our children's calls that trailed behind it.

Maman! Baba! Bastani! Ice cream. Please?!?

We let them run ahead and tried to follow with a light step, but in the end we stood stock-still in the middle of the street, the cold desserts melting onto our fingers and hands as we cried and licked and cried and licked and the salt of tears mixed strangely with the sweet cream.

THE COST OF A TICKET

AFTER A MORNING of walking, Saladin finds the big streets, one after another, an interlocking maze of straight concrete and corners, lampposts and stoplights. It is early. There are few cars and fewer people and he entertains himself with the windows of closed shops and the high, bright billboards. With no map he moves in the direction of the sun's rise as it peaks and shoots out over the eastern mountains, and he does not feel lost. He has taken direction from the sun before. His first day in America and his last day in Istanbul. After the foreman saw their photo on the front page and translated the headline—11 GUILTY KURDS. 3 REVOLUTIONARY GUARDS INJURED, POSSIBLY KILLED. *The Ayatollah has tightened the security presence in the Kurdish region* . . . he told the brothers. *Now you will have to follow the sun* . . . and took Saladin and Ali to a back room where he wrote down an address and a name on a small piece of paper and muttered, We Kurds, always running.

The number was for a dock in the port and the name was of a captain the foreman knew.

He owes me a favor. Tell him Adar sent you. Adar knows the cost. You will be gone from Turkey by nightfall, inshallah. The sun will come up in a few hours, go in the direction of the sunrise. The docks are at the eastern edge of the city.

Saladin took the card. On it, a series of numbers, a name written carefully in block letters and the inky fingerprints of the foreman's stained fingers, whorls that pointed in no direction but circled around and around.

The brothers walked toward the light blue of dawn and then toward the orange of sunrise. They crossed the streets and bridges of Istanbul and did not once ask directions or think they were lost. At the top of a steep hill Saladin insisted they stop and take in the vista, try to use the height to lead them on their way. Around them the city rolled in hills and valleys covered with apartment buildings, parks, minarets and domes. At the far end was a body of water, just as the foreman described, docks full of ships. They rubbed the sweat from their faces and foreheads and walked down the hill with shuffled steps.

Saladin moves across L.A. and thinks, *Are these not the same quick steps? Or are they different steps?* Where he walks now is flat and he is alone. He comes to an area where tall buildings rise up from both sides of the street, the sky above them in a thin blade. He stops to count the windows from sidewalk to roof. Fifteen. Twenty-two. There is one, lean and made mostly of glass, with forty-eight windows from bottom to top. The city wakes up around him and the streets are busier now, the people hurried with their back and forth. He stands before the tallest building he can find and bends his neck all the way back to see the very top windows and cannot help but wonder about their view. He watches people come and go from the revolving doors and knows there is no cost to enter. An old man with a cane smiles at him and this gives him confidence, and soon Saladin is thinking of the many films where Cary Grant or Rock Hudson walks easily into buildings and easily onto elevators, and there is nothing to stop him from being like them, a man in America.

Saladin forgets about his filthy shirt and the sand in his hair and shoes and walks into the marble lobby of the glass building and goes directly to the groups of men and women who wait for the elevator. They smell of ironing and soap and coffee. When the machine comes, he gets on with them, and when it is his turn, he does not push a button. The lift is slight, nothing like the airplane, but his stomach jolts anyway. It stops and goes and stops and empties until Saladin is alone with a short, middle-aged woman with a kind face. She smiles at him and his confidence keeps up and he smiles back. When she gets off, he follows her into a long, bright hallway. The woman turns a corner and disappears, and Saladin walks to the end where a window stretches from floor to ceiling and he takes in as much of the view as he can.

There is the ocean he has just come from, the thin yellow of beach, the ports and piers to the south. There are streets in every direction, highways and freeways lined with buildings. There are whole parking lots filled with the same yellow bus and warehouses without signs or names. There are patches of small homes and lifeless swaths of cement, and the city seems pinned down by billboards and palm trees. Beside him a concrete river cuts through the town, and up above the sky is both blue and brown.

Just as in Istanbul, the vista of Los Angeles calms him. Saladin takes it in like a breath and tries to remember what he sees, the distances between things and the orientation of the mountains to the highways to the seas to the one dry riverbed. He looks straight down to where he just stood and watches the cars and people move about like tiny toys. They move slowly but with purpose, each in its own direction, and Saladin follows one head, a dark, young head of hair just like his, walking down the street. He pretends it is him. That he is a man in a leather jacket with his hands dug deep in his pockets, on his way. The man walks quickly and turns onto a street where most of the buildings have marquee signs, some of them lit and flashing. Not one cinema but a dozen, and Saladin is quick back down the silent hallway where no one has seen or spoken to him, and in front of the elevator again, waiting. He does not know to push a button, and so he waits for five, six, ten minutes until finally a small bell rings and the door opens and a tall man in a suit gets out. Saladin walks in and rides the elevator up for some time, and then, at some point, down.

He finds the street easily, moves slowly past one cinema after another, like a child with a serious choice that matters most and only to him. In one entryway two men approach a glass ticket window and slide money in a thin slit beneath. Two small tickets emerge and the men enter the theater. His confidence fails him and he walks and thinks and walks and remembers all the moments that have required a ticket, all the times on this trip when he and Ali had to pay their way, pay so there might be a way. Low, Saladin walks with measured steps and tries not to look at the glittering marquees, the vivid posters, the happy customers and their pockets of cash.

★ ★ ★

The Istanbul ports were both old and new, and the brothers walked through labyrinths of concrete and rotted wood and shacks that crumbled beside gangly steel machines that lifted incredible weights over busy men with steel hooks in the place of hands.

They found the pier whose number matched the number on the card and saw docked in it a ship of such size that it blocked out the entire horizon behind it. Like a magnet, Saladin moved toward the freighter just to be close to this enormity of metal, to make sure it was, in fact, a boat, and not some steadfast building or steel mountain jutting up from the sea. The ship was tied to the dock by ropes the thickness of a man's arm, and there a group of men had gathered, insignificant, clumped and pacing like confused ants, their faces run through with the same anxiety the brothers would have seen on themselves had they caught sight of their reflection in the water all around. Every man clutched an item. A velvet box. Rugs. Paintings. Copper trays and engraved brass samovars. Saladin stopped as he understood it was not for their human lives or desperate need that they would be allowed on, but for the sake and value of whatever goods they could exchange for another week? month? few years? of life. The spirit that had moved him this far flagged and he took his brother's arm.

Wait, Ali. We have nothing.

Saladin jaan, it is okay. We can always try. Say the foreman's name. And if not, maybe we can find work here, on the docks for a few months. This is enough of a hiding place. It seems far from the city, safe . . .

Ali's voice shook as he spoke. Saladin had never before seen his brother afraid. In their life he was the older, the braver, the one of deep beliefs and great calm, but with each step away from the mountain his brother's noble traits had dimmed and they stood on the docks as near equals. Equally confused before a boat, equally without means and equally exposed on the front page of every newspaper in the city. Ali looked around at the water, the ship, the gathered men, and didn't leave his eyes on anything for too long. The men that milled around them were no more at ease. They smoked nervously and paced restlessly.

What is wrong with trying? They say go eat shit? Then we hide in the docks. The photograph will be garbage in a day. Anyway, the foreman is a Kurd, he would not lead us wrong.

Ali walked toward the waiting men and gestured for Saladin to come stand beside him, and after a time he did. The brothers looked no one in the eye and said nothing. The afternoon heat came and went, and before long the sun fell behind the floating mass of steel and the men grew weary beneath the long shadows of the ship.

At dusk three tan seamen walked down the long, metal plank that lowered from the ship to the ground. The gathered took up their valuables and rushed up to meet them. One of the seamen pulled at the strap of a rifle that he wore diagonally across his back, and the men reversed until they, and their belongings, were on the pier again in three orderly lines, one in front of every seaman.

The brothers chose the line of the seaman with the gun. It was the shortest and the seaman wore sunglasses with silver, reflecting lenses Saladin remembered from a Paul Newman film. When they stood before him, Saladin could see himself as he was, empty-handed, arms stained with ink, scared. He saw his brother beside him, a bit taller, just as dirty, the fear gone from his face. He saw Ali's mouth open calmly and heard his brother introduce himself in a patient, formal Kurdish, and before he was finished, Saladin interrupted him to shout out the foreman's name.

Of the daily paper! Adar! He says he knows the cost.

In the glasses Saladin saw his desperation, the useless gestures of his hands, the way his face pulled in on itself in a confused anger. The seaman did not move and then shrugged his shoulders and raised a hand to rub his fingers against his thumb in a gesture to signify money, payment. Ali spoke calmly.

Adar sent us. He says he knows the cost. Where is the ship going?

Saladin wondered if the seaman understood anything—the Kurdish, the name, their frantic intentions. He got lost in the image in the glasses and for a moment thought he looked handsome and then jumped in surprise as the seaman screamed at them in English and his reflection in the glasses lunged.

No! Go! Enough!

For the first time there was nowhere to go. Behind them an Istanbul covered in newspapers that showed them as accomplices to a massacre; in front of them, the sea. The brothers stood dumbly and the seaman lowered his voice and repeated himself.

Enough. Go. Not allowed.

In the reflection Saladin saw Ali drop his head and push his hand out to the seaman for a shake. Ali cleared his throat and spoke to the man in his most proper English.

Okay. Thank you very much.

And Saladin watched Ali smile, small and quiet, but a smile nonetheless.

It is done, Saladin jaan. We do not have the money, the worth. It is better anyway. We will hide here a few weeks more and then go back. The newspaper will print a different picture tomorrow and soon no one will remember us. They don't even remember us now. Come, jaanam. It is best not to go any farther.

What if someone does recognizes us? Then what? Do we go back to see Baba? . . . It will be bad for us. Terrible. Maybe the ship is safer? Maybe it will take us to Italy? Or maybe London? Then we can go . . .

Ali ignored him and Saladin stopped talking. The man behind pushed the brothers out of the line, and Saladin stood and watched him offer the seaman a tray engraved with a meadow scene. A pair of docile gazelles in tall grasses, a sitting bull under a tree. The seaman inspected the tray and gestured the man to stand beside the ship. Saladin wanted to tell him they could work, on the ship, for the seamen, clean or cook, or wash their clothes, but he knew there was no use in arguments or begging. The truth of their poverty was far greater than his desire. Money. Money. Money. The idea of it tore through Saladin's head and he felt his way through its meaning. A man who wants to look for money, what does he do? Saladin searched his back pocket for a wallet where there was none. He dug his hands deep into the front pockets of his slacks and found lint, a coin of little worth and some hard object with limbs, a head and horns.

Gold.

Saladin removed the figurine and rubbed it between his fingers as if it were the fabled lamp. Without Ali he walked to the silver sunglasses and watched, in their reflection, as the goat expanded and magnified until it took up the surfaces of both the right and left lenses. A thousand years of stubborn gold. The seaman called to the man next to him, and after a second inspection the goat disappeared and the seaman pointed to the small circle of men and valuables.

Go. There. Wait. Today.

Ali spoke up with an angry force.

Where? Where? Wait to go where?

The seaman did not look at Ali, did not cast up his reflective glare for the brothers to see their two faces, one that could not believe his good fortune and one that could not believe his bad luck. The seaman pointed to the circle of men. Saladin grabbed his brother by the arm, and when Ali did not move, he reached for his hand and pulled him. Between their palms Saladin felt both his own terror and Ali's as well.

One question, Saladin jaan, just one question for you.

His brother whispered with a soft, incessant anger.

Why do you think the farther we go the safer we will be? Are we safe in a place where our names mean nothing? A place where we will be no one? Where if we are killed there is no revenge?

If Saladin had known the answer that afternoon, he would have said, *Ali jaan, we are going to America, to California, to Los Angeles, just as Maman would have wanted us to. We can start our lives again there. That is what happens to men in America. You start from nothing and make something. You can be a hero there if you want. I know I will be.* But Saladin knew nothing of that fate or where the boat was going and looked around at the other men for some clue. They stood about, listless and full of nerves, and seemed to care nothing about the where of their journey, only the when. Saladin looked into himself and tried to understand why he was so sure about the boat, its safety and direction. Perhaps Ali was right and it was safer to stay, and when the time came, they could always walk back to the mountain town, face whatever punishment or duty awaited and then sleep in their own beds. The seaman with the silver glasses ordered the gathered men to start up a thin ladder on the side of the ship. Saladin stared at the sunglasses and thought how nice it would be to have a pair for himself.

Ali, it doesn't matter where we go. We can't stay here. Wherever this boat takes us, we will not be as guilty as we are here. We will be strangers, but not witnesses or murderers. We will still be Khourdi brothers. Together.

In saying it Saladin heard a truth that filled him with confidence. Whether from courage or madness or the automatic motion of bodies that had not stopped for days, he pulled his brother tight and near and explained himself like a man who knew more, a man who had lived it all.

If we go back, we will be dead. What good are dead Khourdi brothers? What is the worst thing that could happen? We end up in a strange place? No. The worse thing that could happen is for you to go without me, or me without you. That is the worst thing. Maman and Baba would never forgive us. You carry Kermanshah for me and I carry it for you. When it is time, we will come back together.

Ali was quiet.

A man behind them in line shouted something in an unknown tongue, and Saladin stepped toward the ladder and waited.

His brother stepped forward and took Saladin's shoulder. His eyes were soft and he could not, for a moment, speak.

You may be right. Maybe two Khourdi brothers are better than one. Let us see our fate, Saladin. Let us see what direction we will go and how we will get back.

In the entryway of an extravagant theater Saladin watches a tall, thin man sweep the area in front of the ticket booth. The man sees Saladin and smiles, and Saladin smiles back and the man smiles again, quick and broad, and gestures for Saladin to come, come over. The man has an easy way with his muscles, his arms and legs and face and when he speaks, his voice had so much accent in it Saladin can barely understand. The man takes his shoulder.

Now you go on in. Go on in.

Saladin put his hands in his pockets and looks down. The man squeezes his shoulder.

For free. You go on in. No charge. You look like a nice boy. I am a nice boy too. The film doesn't start for another two hours. I'll see you in there.

Thank you. Thank you very much. It is nice to meet you.

The man continues his sweeping, the smile solid and wide across his face.

In the dimness of his first American cinema, safe in the seat, Saladin lets himself feel the days? weeks? months? as they have accumulated and stressed his body. He kicks his feet up on the chair in front and throws his neck back to stare at the ceiling, and when this is done his body melts a little against the privacy and comfort.

Los Angeles, California, America.

Here.

As long as he could remember it had forever been America and always California, not the Texas of the cowboy movies or the glass canyons of New York, but Los Angeles, and eventually, of course, Hollywood. Others wanted the blond-haired Swedish girls or the fancy Italian Riviera, but Saladin had focused, focused resolutely on one place alone. He remembered the map his mother had ordered from a specialty store in Iran, the way she would point to California and announce, *Children, how I wish I could go and live here. That is where I might be the woman I have always dreamed to be . . . just like Lizbeth Taylor . . .* And then he remembered the small stamp at the end of every film, MADE IN HOLLYWOOD, and the few older high school students who left the mountain town to go to London or Chicago, and how he thought they failed themselves when they could have gone all the way, to Los Angeles. Like this, Saladin lets his thoughts unwind and follows their trail to his first deep, easy sleep. He dreams of his mother, the day the map arrived in the mail. In the dream she spreads the map on the floor and the children gather around to hold down the curling edges. She sits cross-legged and asks, *Where?* The sisters shout, *Kermanshah!*—the only place they know. Ali shouts, *Kurdistan!*—which does not exist. And Saladin shouts, *Los Angeles!* She points at all the locations with red fingernails, the same nails that earned her a black eye from their father, who shouted, *Vanity!* As if it were a place. The children gathered around her in delight. In the dream everyone is the same age, no child older than three or four, and they are giddy with the new game. At one point his mother puts a finger on Los Angeles and a finger on Kermanshah, and Saladin trapezes across arms and shoulders, neck and back, to get from one place to another. Her flesh is slippery beneath his bare feet, and each time he falls, a young, round-faced Ali laughs and says, *Look! Saladin cannot even stand!* Laughs and takes their mother's slaps.

Saladin wakes with the jolt of someone falling in his sleep. The cinema is dark and full with the sound of slow, bare groans. On the screen two men stand, their faces in the same direction, their bodies folded into each other, hips convulsing. There is no music, and Saladin waits for the scene to change, for the story to start, but there is no story, just variations on this one theme, and a dense humidity fills the theater air. Beside him the sweeping man sits and smiles, the broom beside him and his free hand on the top of Saladin's knee. Saladin is quick out of his seat and out of the cinema. His feet take him down busy streets where afternoon light flashes off buildings and blinds him, and he is starving and barely awake and he cannot deny that his second day in America is better than the first, but still, a mixed success.

PATHS, DEPOSITS

THERE WAS NO one path, but the numbers, taken alone, seem to draw a faint line. There is evidence in the documents of the years between 1979 and 1984, and then again in records kept by international refugee and immigrant organizations. If you put them all together and take a close look, it is difficult not to see the pattern emerge.

Turkey: Van, 2,500; Ankara, 3,200; Izmir, 1,800; Istanbul, 10,000 (approx/in transit).

Pakistan: Karachi, 3,500; Quetta, 5,400.

Iraq: Al Basra, 2,200 (approx/in transit).

Greece: Athens, 2,900.

Italy: Rome, 3,200; Turin, 1,500; Milan, 2,000; Florence, 900.

Germany: Frankfurt, 5,200; Munich, 1,200; West Berlin, 2,000.

Holland: Amsterdam, 2,300.

Spain: Madrid, 1,800; Barcelona, 7,000 (approx/in transit).

France: Marseille, 1,100; Paris, 3,200.

England: Manchester, 800; London, 12,000.

Canada: Toronto, 4,800.

United States: New York, 4,500; Washington, D.C., 6,700; Dallas, Chicago, Houston, approx 5,000; San Francisco, 2,000; Los Angeles, 52,000.

They went west. Away from dawn in the direction of night as if the world were a chronometer that rotated from past to present and they walked against what they knew, had known, their childhood worlds behind, before them: the end of day, the soft, unwrit space of night. West. In lieu of a clearly marked path or common route, the storyteller can point to this thin line and say, *This is how it was done, here, this is the way most went. There was a beginning* here (on a map she points to a small nation labeled IRAN) *and for many the end was* here (her finger stretches to the west, across America, to the edge of California, to a LOS ANGELES, a city whose marking falls mostly into the sea).

Yet even the most studious observer of human movement and the most ingenious storyteller cannot say why the Iranian migrants carved a path to Los Angeles. Maybe it is not for the studious or the storytellers to say. Evidence exists, in interviews, official and otherwise.

I had to come here.

My sister lives here.

There was family before here, my uncle visited once, so of course this is where I would end up.

I had a job waiting for me here.

The university gave me a scholarship.

The temperature is perfect. And there are the little red flowers, really that is what made me stay, the tiny, red geraniums that grow off the walls and out of flower boxes, we had these at home. It warms my heart to see them again.

It is most like Tehran, don't you see? To the north the mountains, to the west the mountains, just like the Albroz. And the air! Just the same amount of smog as Tehran!

It is easiest. All kinds are here. We are not the only foreigners.

It seems like the best place.

It is the best place.

It will be the best place. It is right.

What of the answers they did not speak? Those left off the surveys and official accounts? What of the truths buried so deep the migrants forget to mention them to American friends, census takers, refugee organizations, their family, themselves?

We are here because we went to the movies every Saturday afternoon and our eyes took in these buildings, these beaches, these women and men, and we could imagine no other possible home.

We saw it as children, as teens, as young lovers and parents, and that is where we learned to want what we wanted and now what we have come to find for ourselves.

We would have stayed if this was possible at home, but it was not, so we left to seek it out.

We are here because this is the direction the dusty air blew out of the projector and filled the sails of our imaginations.

If the studious observer and the zealous storyteller stay quiet for long enough, they can hear these whispers, echoes of voices that still talk of old movies, old stars, *those Saturday afternoons* at the cinema. This *car.* That *dress. Why can't life be like that here in Tehran/Mashhad/Shiraz/Esfahan?* And if they can keep quiet their noisy, curious heartbeat, they will hear the silence behind all that soft talk, the dead noise of those long lost.

ONBOARD

THE CAPTAIN OF the freight ship wore a linen suit and carried a long, thin crowbar like a cane. He stood to meet the chosen men as they walked up the metal plank and onto a deck no more promising than a cement lot. When they were assembled, he paced before them, swinging the crowbar and speaking in a voice Saladin could barely hear.

This is my ship.

The captain looked at his feet like a man counting his steps.

It belongs to no corporation. No nation. No land and no law. Who you are and why you are here is not my business. I am the captain of a ship that must leave Istanbul tonight and arrive at its destination in no more than two weeks.

His English was like the English of Mr. Hosseini from school, slow and precise, and Saladin thought he understood most of it. He looked around at the twenty or so faces to see what they knew, what they understood, but every expression was the same.

If any of you choose to disturb the process of this journey, the contents of this ship, and I see fit to punish, or even kill you, no one will know, just as no one knows you are here.

The captain went on.

There is no reason for violence. You will be fed once a day. You will be allowed to smoke and walk about. There is an adequate loo but no shower. The forecast is for calm seas, and you are, after all, the fortunate ones. I am sure what has passed and what is to come will not be as easy as this boat ride.

He tapped the crowbar on the cement deck and raised his head. His face was pale and the color of the skin advertised some missing nourishment. He waited and the men rushed to speak, to ask, to demand, but the captain dismissed them with a shaking head.

The destination is not important. We are going west. With any luck you will be closer to wherever you are trying to go and further, inshallah, from here.

The seamen led them to an empty cargo container the size and shape of a boxcar. The door was unhinged, and inside, thin, green military mattresses were strewn about the floor. There were unpaired shoes, newspapers and empty plastic bags with writing in Hindu, Arabic, English and Farsi. Some of the men knew to run to corners or up against the wall to claim the beds farthest from the middle, from the smells and sounds of the other men. Saladin did not know and found a mattress in the middle. He looked to see Ali lie down on another, as far away from him as the shape of the container would allow. The seamen gave instructions in Turkish and left the men alone. The engine started and after some time the ship began to move through the water without opposition or effort.

Many of the men went outside to smoke cigarettes and watch the dotted orange lights of towns on the shores of the Marmara. They floated across a surface without boundaries or borders as underneath them schools of herring and sturgeon swam north with equal ease, seeking out another season in the cold waters of the Black Sea.

Saladin watched the men and the tiny red orbs of their cigarettes bob up and down from their faces like small, bright hearts. They all stayed close beside the hull and avoided the back of the ship from where they could, if they wanted, see the last of Asia. Most looked forward or to the side, and Saladin walked to the far front railing and stared down to the water, which seemed hundreds of feet away, so far he could not see his reflection in it and was left to wonder if he was actually there, on the deck, leaving. In the moonless dark he took in the sea as she showed herself, infinite, dark and extreme, and he wished for Ali to be near, to reassure him, *Saladin baba, don't worry, of course we will find our way back from this.* Time enough passed that the night went from blue to black around him, and when he felt two arms grip him around the chest and throat, there was not enough light to see whom they belonged to. The arms hoisted him up until his knees were level with the highest rail and the heaviest weight of his body was over it and nearly falling down. With the few inches available to him he pushed his elbows out with force, and he heard his brother give a small grunt. The arms threw him to the side and he landed on his shoulder and hip and yelled up at Ali.

Ackmag! What was that?

But his brother was already walking away from him, his back and shoulders set again in the proper lines of his shirt, his swagger easy and his voice light and calm.

Come now, Saladin jaan. Don't you remember? That is how we used to play. I thought I would remind you what its like to have an older brother.

Ali smiled and then laughed.

Relax jaanam, it is no longer up to us. We are afloat to who knows where? We might as well enjoy the ride, no?

During the days the heat in the hull was unbearable. The seas were, as the captain promised, flat, and the only thing that rose up off them was the reflection of the sun. The men did the daily tasks assigned to them and otherwise looked for a cool breeze on deck and the entertainment of one blank horizon after another.

One man had four different passports. Each version had a photo of the same man—small head, flat-line mouth, trim hair and dead expression—beside the official state stamps of England, Syria, Egypt and Germany.

An Afghani man kept dice in one pocket and prayer beads in another. Saladin watched as the man forgot himself and, confused, counted the edges of the dice as he tossed the beads to the ground and took a quick look for some fateful answer.

An Iraqi began his story every time Saladin looked in his direction and stopped, midway, for no reason. The same lines came through his lips each time. I offered, but still they took my family . . . for many months there was not light even . . . at her fourth birthday we had so much money we hired a magician . . . such tricks . . .

The Turkish twins, pacifists escaped from military service, were handsome and fit like warriors. On the sunny afternoons they performed feats of flexibility and strength, juggling cans or holding one another up against the blue blue sky.

A silent group kept to their games of backgammon or cards and did not take part in the fraternity or the play, and a few did nothing more than walk tirelessly through the heat in one lap after another of the ship's oval shape. When Saladin tried to catch Ali's arm and encourage him to *sit* or *rest* or *drink*, his brother shook his head.

I am used to walking now. It is relaxing. Leave me be.

In the heat, or maybe because of it, all the days were the same. The men sweated and waited and sweated more, and by night they were tired and nervous about whatever adventures issued from the dark. One night the ship lost power. The boat sat on the surface of the water and the men took to the deck to play games by the bright moon, and no one said anything about the prison of this sudden stillness. They kept busy with quiet jokes and even quieter cigarettes, anything to distract them from the temptation of the rail's thin edge, the jump in and the swim away.

On another night Saladin woke when the Kashmiri man who slept next to him stepped on his hand. He was in a fight with an Indian man, no more than seventeen or eighteen, and the two pushed and shouted at each other in a girlish way until one of the Turkish twins woke and escorted them outside, where under the immense, empty sky they softened and walked away from one another.

One night the ship docked at a busy island port and the men were ordered off. Many refused, protested that this was not far enough. *We cannot end the trip here! How could this be the last stop?* But the seamen moved them off the ship and into the town, where they followed the captain like punished schoolchildren on a terrifying class trip. Ali trailed far behind and Saladin walked at the very end to make sure that in this new chaos his brother would not let himself get lost.

In a windowless building they went to a room with little ventilation and even less light. In the dim heat women began to appear, one after another after the next and spread themselves about the room without introduction. The captain took his place at a small iron table in the corner and helped himself to an orange from an overfull bowl. Beside him an old woman in a black silk shawl slowly crocheted a black silk shawl.

When the room was full, nearly two women for each man, the captain spit the last of the orange seeds into his cupped palm and announced.

The beauties of Cagliari. Cousins of Sophia Loren. Sisters to Gina Lollobrigida. Take your pick. I will pay. A gesture of goodwill for our journey.

At first no one even looked. The room was stifling with the heat of bodies and the day's leftover temperature. Saladin tried to avert his eyes, but everywhere he moved there was a painted face, a hip or breast or pouf of hair, everywhere flesh: troubled over, overexposed, neglected or too long attended to. Some of them were angels as he had imagined angels—willing, loose limbed, gentle about the face and hands—and some reminded him of sheitans, a constant evil at work behind their eyes and mouths, some hot fire alight deep in the center of their heads. The men shifted and nudged each other, and the women stood perfectly still. Finally the men who coupled with one another in the container every night began to walk the room and pull women to the center, where they grabbed their asses and shoulders and did a coarse dance to the smooth Italian pop that played from another room. Some of the women laughed and others did nothing, and after the dance ended, couples or trios began to disappear down a dark hallway, and soon only a handful of men and a few women were left. Saladin saw his brother on a couch in the far corner, a tall, black-eyed girl on his lap.

In the time after their mother died, the brothers felt what they felt together. Ali would find Saladin and insist, *Let's go for a swim*, and the two brothers walked along the banks of the river to an eddy where Ali would hide behind a boulder and pull Saladin down with him to watch the Kurdish women who lived just outside the town wash their blankets, sheets and each other. For the first few visits there was no desire at the sight of them—sweaty, wet women who laughed and let their hair loose down their backs—and Saladin took in the scene with the same boredom and confusion and sadness that clung to him all the moments after his mother's death. He let himself grow distracted, by the river and the birds and occasionally a girl his age who splashed more than she washed, but mostly he looked at Ali as he pulled at himself rhythmically with what seemed like expert hands, and Saladin waited and ached for his mother in a way that was, at best, painful.

One afternoon, focused on the sight of bare shins and dripping arms and shirts that opened and closed on bare chests, Saladin did as his brother did, and with the sudden release came an understanding, just as abrupt, that those sights produced a hunger that could be fed by the behavior of his hands and body, and, like this, he could carry desire around with him wherever he went. Saladin ran to the cinema and sat for the years of his boyhood and adolescence waiting for bathing suits, silk gowns, tight jeans, underwear, the right kind of T-shirts, to feed this new appetite. He tried to get Ali to come with him, and he did, once, and the brothers sat side by side, and Ali laughed the whole way through a movie with Natalie Wood. *But she is a whore, Saladin jaan. Don't you know? Jeddeh!* After that, Saladin went by himself. He lived his life in game and jest and lust with the girls of the mountain town but saved all of his thickest fantasies for the women that floated off the screen: women with faces as big as buildings, bodies as tall and thin as trees, alabaster skin like poured milk. He imagined taking off their shoes, rolling off the sheer nylons, unbuttoning the skirts or slacks. In some of his imaginings the women were giants and he would climb over their breasts and hips and stand before the center of them, miniature, and take his time walking in. In all of these chimeras he excited himself most with the unwrapping, the slow reveal of this package and all of its heretofore-remote gifts.

The woman who sat on Ali's lap had been unwrapped long ago, some part of her eaten, some already swallowed and a few bits spit out. Saladin tried to see a Sophia or Gina, but in the mud-red dark he saw the face a young girl who knew not what she wanted and the hung skin of a harridan that didn't want anything, anymore.

Ali, what are you doing?

Ali looked at the girl's knees and ran his hands gently between them.

Saladin jaan, why not? It was you who always said an American would be your first. I never said such a thing.

But here? We are almost in America, closer now . . .

Are we? Where are we, brother dear? Tell me so I can find this nowhere on a map. How many days or hours or months should I wait?

The girl ran her mouth against his neck. Her eyes stayed open and stared up at Saladin, feral and black.

Maybe, my brother, tomorrow we will die. Maybe we will die tonight. Shouldn't we take this one pleasure with us?

As if she understood, the woman smiled at the word *pleasure* and kissed Ali's forehead and then his temple. Ali closed his eyes to the touch, and when he opened them, the shade of their green, their stare, was cool and empty.

But what about Heidieh?

Ali lifted and dropped his shoulders. Saladin had never seen his brother so loose, so indifferent and lazy. He had been quiet and far on the boat, and now he was careless and coy. The woman raised herself from his brother's lap, and her head reached much closer to the ceiling than Saladin thought possible. Ali stood shortly beside her, and she took his hand and led him down the hallway, where blackness took the outline of their forms, then the shapes of them and finally the sound of their steps.

Saladin sat alone with the Captain, the old woman, and two whores, one fat with blue eyes and a young woman with tiny teeth in a mouth that didn't close. The room, even in its new emptiness, was warmer than before, and Saladin could smell himself and parts of everyone who had passed through.

Well, Khourdi? You are the shy brother? I wouldn't have guessed it . . .

Saladin did his best to catch the eye of the woman with the small teeth. Though her lips did not press together, she had the face of one without enough air, suffocating. The polish on her nails was chipped, and her hair hung long and limp and thin down her back. And now that it was time for Saladin to do the thing that takes no thought, thoughts came vicious and obstinate: his mother's flesh between her skirt and the short wool sweaters she wore in the winters; Haleh and Heidieh's flesh that wore underpants and undershirts and swam in the river and threw rocks and kept close to him on the hot sand for warmth, their bodies bony and wet; the flesh of his brother when they fought; the flesh of the hands of the dead men, hands he wanted to reach down and hold as they crossed from warm to cold.

The captain winked.

Come, boy. We don't have all night.

Whatever desire Saladin had held in the years since the first desire was now gone. The air in the room grew dense and he sweated at the thought of another's body near his. He craved the cool cinema, the cold women just beyond his reach.

Which will it be?

The captain urged.

Saladin shook his head, little had gone as planned.

No. Merci. No.

Very well.

The captain signaled to the matron in the shawl.

I will take them both.

The two women followed behind the captain as if it made no difference whether they stood or lay down, for whom or how many. He watched the party leave, the backs of the women and their six slow feet, and Saladin knew then it had not gone as planned for the two whores either, and that they were like him, hollow of desire and locked in the not.

For the few hours it took, Saladin stayed in the hot room with the old woman who worked at the silk shawl and did not once meet his gaze. Heat pulsed through all parts of him, and he tried to walk out the same door they all came in, but the door was locked, the old woman useless to his demands to *Open!* In the end he lay in the middle of the floor and waited; never in his life had he been so hot, never had he felt heat for what it was, the body in slow, loud panic, and he would not know it again until his second day in Los Angeles, when he walks under a sun that pushes down and fills him with a slow, steamed dread. He is too nervous to go into the cinemas again and too hungry to stop moving, and he walks about and thinks to find work, thinks of his dirty hands and back and feet, of the days and days of travel that, even after arrival, do not end. His feet move no faster than a shuffle, no faster than those of any animal trapped in a punishing atmosphere.

He walks into an area without houses, grass or bright storefronts. There are no women or children here, only block after block of concrete and cement lots wrapped in chain-link fences, gigantic structures with doors as wide as streets for the groaning trucks and their loads. There are buildings to house the colossal machines that do the work of a thousand hands, buildings that hold no flesh life, only the exchange of labor and steam, electricity and combustion. The warehouses are endless, one after the next, and Saladin stares into the open ones to catch a glimpse of the oiled appendages, the bellies of fire, the miniature men hatted and hard eyed, who rove about to prod and tame and feed the beast. He goes on, past other warehouses closed and dark.

From across the street Saladin sees a line form outside a rolled-up metal door. No sign announces the building or the business, no information explains the amassed, and the line is just a line, twenty or twenty-five men, various in skin and hair, all strong and low to the ground. Saladin walks and stands at the end of it, rests his feet and, for this moment, lets himself belong to something that accepts him.

The line moves in one-person increments, and Saladin does not speak to the man in front of him or the man behind him. The sun beats down over their dark heads, and one by one they disappear into a room under the rolled-up metal door. Some reappear with papers in hand, some without, but all wear a wet sheen across their faces as if whatever trial they went through in the office of the enormous building was even hotter than the trial of the sidewalk or the street. Saladin shifts his weight from one foot to another, moves the few inches forward and expects nothing.

When he is near the front of the line, he sees a small office with a glass window in the door. The man in the office gestures for the next in line, and the stocky man in front of Saladin goes in and closes the door behind him. They sit in an almost silence, punctuated by occasional movements of the lips and nods. All around them, inside the office and out, a horrible noise churns in the air—pneumatic hisses, collisions of metals. The sensation is that something tremendous is either dying or being born.

You ever work steel before?

Saladin understands the word work, thinks of the money he does not have on his second day in America and how soon, on the third and fourth and fifth and thousandth day, he will need money to eat, to be left alone, to live. He thinks of the hunger he felt this morning and just a few minutes ago. He nods to the man's question.

Yes. Work.

You know your way around a crucible?

He knows if he answers in the affirmative the back door of the office will be opened and he can go to the place where the work is, where he is given the papers in the hand and can wear the nervous, resolved look that will make him one of them, a worker. He nods once more and, to make sure, mutters, *Yes.* Yes, because more than the work Saladin wants to see the machine, this machine that breathes and spits just behind the office door.

We pay cash. Two weeks on Friday.

Yes.

The foreman stares at him for a second after his answer and then another long second after that. Saladin cannot tell if he is skeptical or if the narrow look is simply his regular face. His eyes are small and set far back into his head. On his forearm a faint anchor is tattooed, beneath the anchor another tattoo, even more faint.

Let's go have a look. I'll know when you see her if you've ever seen her before.

The man is slow and patient in his movements and turns the doorknob with impossibly swollen fingers on an impossibly swollen hand. They walk out the back door of the office into a warehouse with windows high, almost too high to let in any light, and hot. Ash and dust cover everything and Saladin lets his eyes adjust to the dimness until only one thing is in front of him: a stove the size of a house, black encrusted on the outside and with the red glow of a giant's hearth within; the source of all heat and noise; the behemoth. The men that work it are small and sweating and all of them in the same service. Now and again one of them opens a large metal door, and Saladin can see the tense, white heat at the center of the oven and the molten iron around it.

She holds thirty-two tons of oxidized steel.

The foreman walks toward the heat and Saladin knows to follow, knows this is the test, the trial that determines him as capable or not in this man's world, as a worker here or wanderer on the streets. In the oven the crucible does not glow. It takes the fury of the heat that surrounds it, burns beneath, melts through, and stores it, conforms and contorts so that one element may change into another. Saladin stands as close to the insurmountable heat as he can bear. He breathes through his mouth because it burns to inhale through his nose; his clothes absorb the water that pours from him. In a moment he too will melt, leaving only the essential elements of his human form: the calcified teeth, the belt buckle, the bones and the fundamental ash: resistant; age-old; our common element. The foreman takes a step closer to the oven, his skin and T-shirt parchment dry, hands in his pocket and a proud push in his chest. He talks to the noise of the oven, to the hotbox and fire.

It is the heat that breaks it, takes the pieces apart, all the earth spent so long pushing together. You get the temperature up high enough and you can undo all that and then there is just steel. Strong steel.

He takes a step closer and Saladin tries to follow, to keep up, but the heat singes at his shirt, and the polyester of his pants from the tailor in Tabriz sizzles and his skin is on fire beneath it. Nothing about him can withstand the furnace before him, but he nods yes. Yes. Yes. Even though he understands nothing. Not the chemistry. Not the piercing heat in his lungs. Not the foreman's words or the work of the machine. In the presence of the fire he only recognizes fire. The heat that keeps him at bay, that asks no permission to take him apart, melt him into an anonymous version of himself. When the foreman turns to look back at him, Saladin's face and hair and shirt and shoes are wet.

The foreman laughs and the edges of his lips lift.

Thought so.

The foreman walks to the back door of the office, holds it open for Saladin and without a handshake opens it to the street and lets Saladin out in a gesture that lets the next man in.

The air on the street is only slightly cooler; Saladin can breathe it, see through it, just barely think in it, and he walks away from the warehouse and the slow-moving line of men who come to wait and then work and then dissolve into component parts in service to the steel.

By afternoon he has made his way downtown among the vendors and the tall buildings, and still the heat is inside him, a steady, strong burn that emanates from the gut, fills the nodes of the spine and glows throughout. Around him the city holds her own heat: the sharp blades of light reflect off the glass of skyscrapers, the cars and sewer grates and chrome, and over them the sun caresses it all. Though he walks and walks, Saladin finds no relief from mountain grass or cool rivers; there are only boulevards lined with desiccated plane trees, their bark drier than the inside of his mouth. He cannot think of a time when this slow walking will ever end.

He stops at a truck that sells food from a window in its side and watches the men order and then does the same as them. He holds up two digits, and when the food comes, the tortilla and the meat and the sprinkling of onions and cilantro, he runs away and the man in the truck shouts and then shakes his head but stays trapped in the truck. Moving, Saladin takes a bite and is burned by the hot oil of the meat, and the vendor—a melted man who sits in an aluminum truck in front of a hot stove under the hot sun and bakes himself each day—sees the thief suffer and laughs. The vendor's laugh, the spit and sound of it, travel out from the little window of his truck and attach themselves to Saladin, who is molten and sticky and takes to him everything he encounters, for the heat has eroded the defense of clothes, of fear, ideas or determinations. He sees the tears drop from his eyes, warm and salty, and watches as they become a part of the Los Angeles sidewalk. He runs and bites and chews, finishes the food, tastes nothing of it and moves on.

Like this the afternoon passes. The city gathers enough heat to melt all people into their constituent parts: the lips of smiles, the tremble of laughs, the blink of eyes, drops of sweat, the scent of fear or exhaustion or lust, chords of a call, the touch of hands and shoulder and hips in passing. Everything comes apart, attaches to everything else, seeks shade, cools and becomes anew, a little bit less of itself, a little more of the whole.

Saladin sits on a bus stop bench next to a Chinese woman in white pants and thick-soled shoes and a nurse's cap. For a brief moment their thighs touch, and she leaves something of herself on his pliant body and he moves on. On a street where people sleep on stacked cardboard boxes, a man with a halo of white hair and dry, black skin comes from behind and slaps his damp shoulder. *Hey, man! Hey! Hey, man!* Saladin keeps moving but the man's handprint is still there, on his shoulder, like a stamp. Across the street a girl runs from her brother and into the traffic. Her small body narrowly misses the bumpers of cars that honk furiously and brake with even greater fury. Behind her, a mother shouts and drivers shout and her brother laughs and the girl runs to grab Saladin by the leg. Her body, as tall as his knee, shakes, but she smiles up at him in a delirious terror. The mother pries her off, and the shape of her plump arms and small hands leaves a ring around Saladin's thigh. *Yes. Yes. Yes.* He takes it all, lets the mold change shape, and moves his supple figure around the boulevards and alleys downtown and yields to it all—the games of children; the scowls of the old men gathered around dominoes; the confusion in the eyes of the men and women like him, just arrived; the mother's frustrated yell; the empty hands of beggars that open and close and send all their want up into thin air. *Yes. Yes. Yes.* He has no choice, cannot, by strength of will, resist. The city is a furnace and the human elements therein crumble in the fire, morph into one another and so create a new element that belongs more to Los Angeles than to whatever oven held them before.

WHAT THEY DO

AT FIRST THEY cannot work. In the early days and first weeks all they can do is keep their heads above the surface of this new reality of Los Angeles. Once they take the first easy breath, eat the thick meal that reminds them of home, find their minds bored, the men slap palms to thighbones and announce.

We must work.

We have not come all this way to sit in the sun.

And like that the men and women of the migration determine to belong and a job will help make it so.

The ones who did it all—carpentry, construction, tailors, cabdrivers, repairmen—before, do it all here. When they show their faces at the jobs that require no faces, the bosses and supervisors take one look at their rocky knuckles and thick wrists, the brawn of their forearms or the skill in their fingers, and nod. They may ask a few questions, wonder if it is a Mexican, an Egyptian, a Pakistani or a

Greek that stands before them, but they don't ask. When they cannot decide, the foremen look back at the worn fingertips and diligent eyes and nod yes, and just like that the ones who did it all before do it all here, and the machinery of the city takes them in.

The ones who did something in the bazaar, whose little shops traded wholesale in antiques, jewels, spices, rugs or brass, arrive in Los Angeles, Glendale, or Santa Monica to open the very same stores they had closed just last month, last year, in Tehran, Shiraz and Tabriz. In the corner of these new old shops a samovar is always hot, and the voice of a woman dying for love floats out of an old cassette player that never turns off. The rug and spice stores smell so much like home that customers stand around for hours and forget what they had come for in the first place. They trade in whatever they can get—appliances, furniture, kitchenware, fabric—and turn no customer away, glad as they are, these ageless, placeless merchants, to wake up in the morning and have a trade to make.

For those who did one thing, they come to find that here they can do little or, at first, nothing at all. They had given years of study and thought to the structures of bridges, the formation of law, the mechanics of the heart's valves, and yet here their steady knowledge is not enough. Of those who did one thing, many come to Los Angeles only to realize they must learn to do it all. They take positions behind trucks, in grocery stores, at dry cleaners and gas pumps and say nothing about their fine and useless skills, so great their shame and eventual defeat. One man, an engineer from Mashhad, worked at a mechanic shop on Wilshire for six months and complained to his wife that of all the annoyances in his new life, the engine grease that stayed underneath his fingernails was the most insulting. She may or may not have comforted him, and the next day he woke with even less enthusiasm for this new world. Another man, it is said, dressed the part of a lung surgeon and went to the hospital every morning, where he emptied bedpans and trash bins and then committed a meticulous suicide.

For those who did bad things, the worst things or nothing at all in the face of the Shah's desperate repressions, work was irrelevant. They saw their names on the death lists and simply escaped with no plan other than that. Some try their hand at this or that, real estate, banking, restaurants, but most sit back, smoke their cigarettes and look out over Los Angeles from balconies up high. A few forget themselves, grow successful in various businesses, work day and night for an income that keeps coming, that keeps the nightmares of before back. They pay their taxes, apply for citizenship, go to jury duty and take their happy families for long walks on the clean beaches in Malibu or Santa Monica, where if some acquaintance from the old country and old life recognized them and called out—*Captain! Lieutenant! Sergeant!*—they would not answer, they would not even turn their heads.

At first the women do as most of them did before. If they stayed at home with the children, they do the same here and live the lives of mothers and wives, keep kitchens clean and warm and noses dry. If money starts to run short, some of the women offer to work, only to hear the deafening protests of their husbands and fathers and brothers.

Bravely they retort.

Why not? The Amreekaye women do it. So can we.

With their little English they find themselves at grocery stores, preschools, the perfume counters of JCPenney or Macy's, where they smile and spritz and wonder, *What is so bad about this life? I have a little money every month, strangers are nice to me, I meet Americans. It is better than sitting at home.* If they have considerable English, they take jobs as loan officers, bank tellers and teachers. Some even go to university and come out as architects, nurses and professors, and with each paycheck in the bank everything they have known before changes. Each time they buy a new pair of shoes with their own money or take a compliment from their boss, the world shifts a degree or two in orientation and shade and they can barely believe how big their life has become.

Until they take the weekly phone calls from back home, the women in America forget that things can change for the worse as well. They listen to their mothers and sisters and best friends, the chorus of old loved voices now beset by hysteria.

You know what they are shouting now?

Roosari ya tusari!

A head scarf or a blow to the head! They are shouting this to our faces when we walk to school. We have to sit in the back of the bus! Do you know this! Can you believe it? Even the cinema it is split, men on one side, women on the other . . .

The voices on the phone go on appalled, reined in only by pauses of disbelief that are broken to ask again and again.

Can you believe it?

Can you?

The women in America hold on to their phones and shake their heads but say nothing. When the conversations end with their ancient farewells of *God be with you* and *My soul will die for you*, the women in America return to lives where the days are long and exhausting and mix all the new chores of work and traffic and customers with the old chores of cooking and children and tea, and they keep at it, diligent, and remind themselves, *We did not come here to sit in the sun.*

HUNGER

THE FIRST DAY of foul weather pulled the men apart. They stayed away from the groups and the games and kept to themselves under deep and roiling skies. Saladin climbed to the top of a stack of containers to watch skies that had so far been open and blue turn gray and churned. He watched the sky until he grew tired and then watched the deck, where the captain paced at the door of their sleeping container, back and forth, hitting the cement with his crowbar at even intervals. For every two steps he tapped his crowbar *tock*, and the rhythm drew the men out from their moody distances. Saladin climbed down from his perch and stood beside his brother, who, for once in all the boat days, did not move away. The captain walked and spoke.

We are between sixteen and eighteen hours from our arrival, depending on the weather. You must be in the container at dusk. That is when we will close and seal the door in preparation for arrival, for your safety.

Tock. Tock.

Here you will wait. One night and a morning will pass before we dock. There are vents cut into the ceiling, but I suggest you keep still, do not argue or smoke too much. There will be enough air, but just enough.

Tock. Tock.

They will search the boat, container by container, and they have, in the past, opened them. They can be lazy too, on these islands especially. They don't have the police of Rome or Nice or Lisbon. There should be no dogs . . . I have done this for your sake.

Tock. Tock.

The captain went on. He told them the story of the night they had yet to live, explained the search, the shipyards, their exit from a high door in the ceiling where a rope ladder hung. The men who understood all of the captain's English kept drawn faces, and the men who understood less mimicked the dread.

Tock. Tock.

Alone or in pairs from the small door in the ceiling. But not until night, wait until at least late afternoon or night.

They watched the captain go, and Saladin felt a hand on his shoulder.

Ali did not seem scared. His posture was fallen like that of a man who didn't mind what happened to him, one way or another.

Saladin jaan, what do you think now? Should we keep going forward, keep on, right into our big metal coffin?

The men stayed outside the container until the rains came. They kept themselves busy with their second, fifth or twelfth cigarette as a brisk wind flapped at their collars, lifted and dropped their oily hair. To ease their nerves the Turkish brothers took turns holding themselves perfectly upright, perfectly upside down in long handstands off the railings, nothing but air between their backs and the far, whitecapped seas below. Saladin sat at a distance and tried to see a tomorrow for them all, a day in the sun, on land, in their next destination, but all he saw was a bruised sky that swirled above a gathering of tiny, nervous men. He closed his eyes and tried to avoid the one thought that plagued him, that came and went, came and went, circling his consciousness like carrion. *Brother, have I come to kill you? Brother, have I come to kill us both?*

Some men ate from nervousness and the seamen chided them.

I wouldn't take that last bowl of rice, especially with the doors closed.

The men who made a practice of walking around the ship were forced by the weather to sit in the container and wait. Saladin found his brother in a corner, beside a middle-aged Afghani man who showed him pictures of his family, his life.

This is my daughter, and here with my wife. My mother. Noruz. And my other daughter. Can you believe that? I am a man with six sisters! A curse of women, I used to joke . . . Ay Khoda, I used to joke. And you? Your family? Where are your photos?

I have no photos.

Ah.

I left by accident. It was not planned.

The Afghani man nodded his head.

And now what? Where do you go now?

Ali smiled.

I am going to the same place you are going.

The Afghani ignored the dark meaning and continued on.

Ah. And your brother?

My brother . . . I do not know where my brother is going.

Ah.

Saladin pretended not to hear it, and soon the container began to reek of cigarettes and sweat and he left. He walked, oblivious to the rain and the rough seas, along the long hallways of the ship and searched for the entrance to the small, three-story building that rose up from the deck. He knew it was where the seamen and the captain slept, where they kept the better food and the instruments that navigated the boat. He walked from one landing to the next until he came to an open door, knocked on the doorframe and looked in. Old silk rugs hung on the walls in sheets, samovars of engraved brass and copper were thrown to corners and wooden crates were full with gold picture frames, watches and ugly antique jewelry. In the corner was a box of small, bejeweled eggs. The captain sat at a desk next to a window and let the rain pelt the maps and charts spread in front of him. He cradled a half-empty bottle of a burgundy liquid and called out to Saladin.

Come in, Khourdi! Come in!

Saladin sat on the edge of a bed bolted to the floor. The captain held out the bottle and then reconsidered and offered nothing. In a rough, clear Farsi he finished a sentence out loud that seemed to have started in his head.

. . . after so many years, her moods are my own. She has a bad day and I do too.

The ship tilted heavily and the captain raised the bottle.

Let me not pretend to do God's work. I am Cato the boatman, no more, no less. I move those who must be moved, those who seek me out, pay me, and they agree to be locked up for a night, their own free will . . . I ask no questions, think nothing of the horrible things they might have done, or that have been done to them, or the desperation, if they are murderers or . . . or . . .

His head tipped lightly against his chin and his eyelids fell, and the contortions of his face eased until he looked like the glad captain from the whorehouse and then like a young man and finally, with a line of spit falling from his mouth, like a baby. Saladin felt himself nervous now, eager and ill at ease. He leaned into the sleeping man's ear and listened to the shallow breath, smelled the rot of fermentation and cigarettes, and when he was sure the captain was asleep, quietly he confessed.

I was forced to take the gun. I was my father's son. He was told by the mullah to gather the guilty, arrange a trial . . . an execution, to show his loyalty. Eleven men. Kurds I knew. The mullah ordered the guns fired, and just like that the men were dead. Almost dead. When I shot again, I might have killed them. My brother shot three guardsmen. They fell. We escaped into the mountains, my brother and I.

He waited to see if the captain would wake.

My father is a coward. I was too.

With each word a bit of his old actions unbuckled inside until he felt neither badly nor right, but without blame. He leaned back and tried to speak loudly.

But I am not a coward tonight. I have always wanted, more than anything, to go to America. We are going to America. My brother, Ali, and I. We are brave to do it. Heroes.

The words sounded strange when he said them, like false declarations, and Saladin felt a tickle in his spine, at the back of his eyes. He approached the sleeping form and carefully took the bottle from the crook of the captain's arm and drank from it until it was empty. The liquid stung his throat and chest, and when the sensations calmed, he tucked the bottle underneath one of many silk pillows and left.

The rain was a soft drizzle now and Saladin went to the railing to clear his head and steady his stomach. He was joined by the middle-aged Afghani man, who stood pensively beside as the ship tossed lightly beneath them. The man took long, deep breaths, and Saladin thought to imitate him, thought the man must know something about putting a mind at ease, but after two breaths he vomited out all he'd drunk. The man patted his shoulder.

You will be fine. We all will.

The Afghani man kept his hand on Saladin's shoulder.

I have made this trip before. I have been to America. You will be treated well there. Work will be easy, you will save your money, a house will come, no one will bother you, and then it will be time to go home again. Inshallah.

Rain pelted their faces and the man squinted as they spoke. Saladin had many questions. Why did he go back? Why was he here now? Where should they go when they first arrive? How much does a car cost?

You have been to America?

Yes.

Where?

California.

Saladin had nothing to say after that. The man's body and voice and heartbeat was evidence enough that the journey might not end in death, that Saladin and Ali might survive.

And you are going back? Now?

Yes.

And there is work there, a life. Cars?

The man nodded and looked out over the ocean's rough waters.

You and your brother will be okay. Go together, find a new life. And one day, God willing, you can go back home.

When the seamen made their call, Saladin found Ali cross-legged and eyes closed on his thin mattress.

Ali.

Yes, jaanam.

We are going to be fine.

We shall see, jaanam. We shall see.

The Afghan has been to California. He told me about it. He said life there was easy. There was work. Good places to live. Cars for everyone. We will be fine. And when the time comes, maybe we can even come home!

The doors were closed, and in the darkness the men could hear the banging that sealed them. Saladin felt a solid hand on his knee, familiar and forceful.

We shall see, Saladin jaan. We shall see.

Saladin took from the voice what he needed: a sound from home, the known language, the tone he had known his whole life. He sat shoulder to shoulder with his brother, closed his eyes and waited for the end of a night that would, in one manner or another, move them onward, move them out.

The storm did not reach them immediately. Most of the men fell asleep only to awake, a few hours later, in a world where there was no brother and no stranger and they moved in the hull as one. The jolts got worse until they could get no worse, and each time Saladin thought it could get no worse, every heave was higher, every toss and slam more painful and unexpected. There was no up or down, and the flesh of one man crashed into the bones of another, and everything that was in the container mixed until there was just one scream and one bruised body and one worried heart among them all, and they moved across the angry waters as any flock or herd or school in motion moves, indistinguishable and en masse.

Saladin did not seek out his brother. He let other hands grip him, took other flesh into his hands and embraced as turbulence rocked the container so hard he could no longer recognize himself or call out to Ali uniquely, and the nameless force of death played with all the men as if they were a man.

After a time not made of seconds or minutes, each toss and slam was less, each terrible motion half the one before, and then half of that, until the ship rocked side to side like a paper boat in a light wind. In the stillness Saladin sat with his back leaned up against an unknown back and listened to the silence. He knew they were all glad for the darkness that hid them from one another, hid the shame they shared for the ways they had cried and begged and clutched at one another, for the ways in which they were weak.

Saladin did not search for his brother and held to himself and cried for fresh air, for a river, for a woman, for all he had planned for himself before he died. He sat starving for life, for a taste of what he could have if the world made itself available to him for just one more day of sky, water and rocks. He sat in the rancid dark of men and bodies and thoughts of death and could not quiet his famished soul. The hunger was too great. He tried to busy himself with thoughts of tomorrow and America and the next cinema, but he was weak and came apart easily at the end and split down the middle, one half of him craving life and the other half tired for a sleep beyond sleep.

On his third day in America Saladin wakes with the same stomach of acid and bile. He is covered in an unfamiliar blanket and does not know if the memories of the men locked and tossed were a nightmare of this recent sleep or some tragedy from another world. He pretends the blanket is his own, that something is his, and tries to get comfortable beneath it, but the scents are too many and keep his brain busy with their puzzles. Motor oil, sweat and old feces and then, below it all, burnt sugar from a cake or cookie. When he catches this scent, Saladin holds to it like a dog and sniffs out the blanket for more, maybe something cooked, maybe meat, and his hunger swells and there is no more reason to smell what he can't eat, and he stands up and searches his pockets for the nothing he knows is in them and imagines the bread he will buy, the egg plate he watched an old lady eat at a diner, the possibility of food.

With empty hands and nowhere to go, he kicks the blanket until the gray wool mass and all its thousand smells are partially buried in the sand. He goes to the water and washes his hands and face in the salty foam and walks east into the city. It is early yet and already this day is longer than the rest.

As it was with his few American days before, it is today again: Saladin cannot find the city itself, the core of polished steel and elegant women and invitations from tall, suited men to *come* and have a meal, a seat, take this job, this money, this dream. He ambles through the early-morning fog with no sense of direction and tries his best not to think, Who has ever been this hungry? Who, in the American movies, has ever been so lost? He moves up Venice Boulevard and recognizes the few landmarks he knows, the cinema that is closed and broken, the storefront that advertises headless mannequins in costumes of strapped leather and spikes, the big, blue Dumpster where, just yesterday, he watched a bearded, blond man dig through to find and eat hunks of bread, halves of sandwiches, a bitten apple. Saladin's stomach cringed at the sight, but he stared anyway, and the bearded man noticed him, laughed and rubbed his stomach like a sated king. Today Saladin walks past them all, turns in an unfamiliar direction and pushes himself to go, go on.

By midday the clouds tear apart and the great heat starts to seep into the city. Saladin is in a hilly neighborhood where the curbs are swept and palm trees grow in long, straight lines and the women trail tiny dogs on leather leads. The order of this world is the order of the world he knows from the movies, even, clean and without haste, and he tries to feel arrived, tries to relax into this setting, but the hunger burns holes in his stomach and he feels his spine fold down, his shoulders stiffen, and his feet take only the smallest, angriest steps.

At an intersection where two gas stations face each other, Saladin watches a man with his age and color and hairstyle run to meet each car as it drives in. He greets the drivers with a tremendous smile and then rushes to stick the nozzle into their cars, clean the windows and check the oil as the drivers sit, fix their hair and pick their noses. When it is done, Saladin sees the easy exchange of money from driver hand to attendant hand, and he thinks about it. Fast. Little talking. Many cars. Cash. The light changes and Saladin lifts his heavy feet to cross the street. On the other side a tall girl with her hair nearly white from the sun smiles as she walks past him in the opposite direction. Her dress is long and thin and light in the wind and sun, and he turns to find her figure is nearly visible beneath it. She floats away from him, and whatever parts of her he cannot see, Saladin makes up and remembers he did not move to America to work at a gas station.

He walks a long distance to the east and the hunger comes and goes in episodes, each new issue sharper and more relentless. He stops to sit frequently, and on one shaded bench he stays long enough for his heart to finally steady. An odd calm comes over him, its edges tinged with euphoria. In a schoolyard across the street the children are busy on playground swings with games in cement squares, competitions with balls and hoops. They are various in color and age, but divided evenly into groups of boys and girls. At the far edge of the yard some play a game of running and touching and standing frozen, and closer to him a pair of girls sit across from each other and sing a rhyme over the intricate rhythms of their fast-clapping hands. Saladin sees boys he could have been and boys, lonely and preoccupied, that could be him. They are schoolchildren just like the schoolchildren in the mountain town except that a few of them are very fat, larger than children as he remembers them. Saladin leans against the bench and gives himself over to their games with such pleasure that when a boy with tight, curly hair scores in the game of the ball and high net, Saladin has to stop himself from standing up to cheer.

At intervals the students are called to gather. They form lines, and one group leaves the yard as another group comes on. In the new group everything is the same as the last with the exception of two overly large boys, no more than eleven or twelve, who forgo the games to walk the perimeter of the yard slowly and without purpose. One eats small, triangular crisps out of a bag, and the other sucks on a candy fastened to a stick. When they near him, Saladin tries his best not to stare, but he cannot look away from the fat of their faces and necks and small, bloated hands. The calm is gone now and Saladin watches the two as they eat slowly and without end and lets the hunger gnarl in his gut and malice fill his head, and he would like nothing more than to climb the fence into the yard and take the crispy snack from the boy and then lick the salt off each salty finger and perhaps eat the finger itself.

He stands to leave and his head spins in a thousand directions, and he forces himself, with the help of the bench, to move out into the sun, where he is nearer to the boys, who are now stopped so the one can swallow the remaining contents directly from the bag and then toss the bag onto the grass, where the wind fills and lifts it off the ground.

The boy, no longer distracted by his food, looks over at Saladin and shouts.

Hey, faggot! What are you staring at?

The two boys laugh and turn their back to him, and Saladin walks away, his steps neither quick nor proud.

He must breathe. But when he does, the smell of meat fills his nose. He tries to stand away from the building it comes out of, to stop his inhales so he can stop the smell and so stop the hunger. With held breath he stands on the sidewalk and thinks about death for the first time in his American life. He stares at the busy street beside him and sees his own body in the gutter, flat out, his hair and hands and feet loose as if they were under water. He goes to touch his forehead, and his hand feels only concrete and a copper coin under his finger. He exhales and takes up the coin, bites it to see if it is true or, like his laid-out death, a fantasy of his dire imagination. It is real and he takes it his hand and walks quickly toward the smell of kebab that maddens him.

All along the front of the building are windows, and everyone eats outside beneath a large metal shade or on picnic tables in the sun. Saladin looks twice, and it is as it is in the movies with the *hamburgers* and the *french fries*, and all that is missing are the girls on roller skates and the music. But the smell that was never in the cinema is here now, and it draws him as it is food and fat and salt and oil, and with hunger as his only imperative he walks to a window with a square cut out of it and announces himself.

Hello. My name is Saladin. One hamburger, please.

The man behind the glass is black skinned and wears a stiff, white paper cap. He writes something on a small sheet of lined paper and then looks to Saladin.

That's a dollah twenty-five.

— — —

I said, that's one twenty five.

Saladin produces the penny, and the young man laughs and calls to another young, black-skinned man and the two stand there passing the coin back and forth and laughing. They call another, and a man emerges from the back, darker and older.

One of the young men holds up the coin.

We got a Mexican here trying to pay us a penny.

He turns to Saladin.

You know this is a penny, right?

Saladin does not move.

The old man, his hair white at the tips as if dusted with ash, looks at Saladin and then at the coin.

Giver here.

He takes it, rubs it with the corner of his apron, and puts it in his pocket. Then he rests his eyes on Saladin as if he can see all that is behind and around and in front of him.

Where you from?

— — —

Where are your people?

— — —

The old man turns away and shouts over his shoulder to the younger workers.

Give him a couple of cheeseburgers with bacon, fries, and a shake. You like shakes or sodas?

The younger boys shake their heads as if they cannot believe it.

Give him a shake. Chocolate.

For his fortune a box full of food appears, and Saladin eats like an addict, beyond his fill, desperately and without thought. When he stands to leave, the street blurs and his feet are not lighter or stronger for the nourishment. The afternoon is hot now and he makes a sluggish exit out of the parking lot, down a busy street where even the noise and speed of cars are muted by this sudden fullness. His stomach churns, and by the end of the second block he vomits in front of a store full of washers and dryers. He vomits again and the street ignores him. When he is empty he stands straight, spits and marches forward, light now and wanting only a glass of cold water.

He walks down streets of endless parking lots, strips of stores, gas station after gas station. He holds an old woman by the arm as she crosses the street and explains, as she tries to shake him off, that his own mother considered him a gentleman and it was only right . . . The Farsi frightens her, and when they are on the sidewalk again, she walks briskly away from him. Saladin nurtures his good mood and lets himself smile at women, young and old, and he looks nobly at the strange men who might one day be his boss, brother or friend.

You ever lift a pump before?

He is at his fourth gas station of the day. The manager looks at him directly. When there is no answer, he repeats the question.

You ever lift a pump?

At the first station Saladin lied when the manager asked, *Ever done it?* At the second station he rushed to prove himself and stood beside the pump until a car arrived, and he faked expertise with the cap and the nozzle and the latch, only to end up covered in gasoline. One after another the managers dismissed him with little more than a wave of the hand.

The third manager, a Chinese, refused to let him even touch the pump.

No. No. You are too dirty. Too smelly. Your clothes, a mess.

Saladin looked down to the center of his chest where the short man was pointing and knew what he meant. He had not taken anything more than a sea bath, and if he held his fingers to his nose he could still smell the island. No arrogance or imagination could sidestep the truth of his filth: he was a man without a home who had pissed between parked cars and in alleys and had not yet, from lack of food or fear, taken his first American shit, and for this he felt all the more soiled.

Well? Have you?

The manager asks again. He is an old man with a half crown of white hair below his ears and a bulbous nose, red and inflated.

Yes. Every day. Professional.

Saladin walks to the pump, pulls the nozzle out and lifts the latch. There are no cars but he stands there anyway, nozzle up in the air, waiting. He gives his best cinema smile, and the manager lets out a chortle.

All right, all right. You look professional enough. Lucky for you I had my guy quit on me just this morning. Niggers. That's what you get for being an equal-opportunity employer. Come on in and we can fill out the paperwork.

The office has a cash register, quarts of oil, washer fluid, candy and gum. From habit Saladin looks around for bread, cheese, something he can buy as soon as the old man pays him for the first day's work. Sandwiches, days old, taunt him from a small glass refrigerator. He puts his hands in his empty pockets and does not look around anymore.

The manager slides a piece of paper across the counter.

Here. Fill this out.

He pauses and looks long at Saladin, who has not yet spoken.

I bet you can't even speak enough English for that. That's all right. I'll help you out. Hell, I done it for the last three guys . . . Lemme find a pen.

The man bends down to dig in the bottom drawers of a creaky desk, and over the arch of his back a small, black-and-white television flicks a rolling image into the small room. On the screen an anchor with slicked-back hair stiffly holds a few sheets of paper and speaks without moving the muscles of his face. Behind his perfect, immobile head is a map of the Middle East. Saladin recognizes Iran from its shape and because it is the only nation highlighted in white, the surrounding countries left shaded and nameless. In an instant the man and the map disappear and are replaced by images of a square in Tehran where men and women chant in groups and a parade of captives marches slowly through the center of them. Saladin recognizes the place and sees that the faces of the protesters are Iranian faces and that the eyes of the forty or fifty or fifty-two men are covered by wide, white blindfolds no different from the blindfolds knotted at the back of the heads in that green valley, long ago.

Yet somehow long ago is not long enough, and Iran is in Los Angeles, and at this very moment the fifty-two captives parade around the gas station convenience store where an old man searches for a pen. Just like that Saladin is both in California and also in the Tehran square, standing between a cloaked woman and a young father with his son on his shoulder, his ears deaf from the shouts of *Marg! Barg! Amreeka!* He is staring at the television at the gas station and he is staring at the mullahs in the square who float, gray robed and severe, just as the mullah in the valley floated, and then it is only a matter of seconds before he is sure that the blindfolds on the fifty-two captives are the exact same as the eleven blindfolds bound on the men in the valley, washed and reused for the purpose that makes one blindfold exactly the same as the other: to block sight; place a thin layer between the known and unknown; form a membrane through which one may be accused and punished and seen but not receive the same in return.

Behind the counter the old man bends and mumbles, and the news plays on behind his back. The crowds chant.

Marg barg Amreeka!

The square-faced announcer translates.

In a second day of protests crowds have gathered in Azadi Square to shout "Death to America" and show their support for Khomeini and his fifty-two American hostages captured at the American embassy only one week ago. It appears that the hostages have been brought here to walk around Azadi Square, perhaps to demonstrate their good health in continuing captivity.

Time and space fold on themselves, and Saladin is confused by questions. When did they gather in the square? Does the television show this exact moment or a moment yesterday? Last week? And if this moment is now, how can that be? And if it *is* now, then what of this journey, these weeks of walking and flying and swimming? Did it happen? Have I escaped enough or not? If I was a guilty man *there*, am I guilty *everywhere*?

I had a damn pen just a minute ago . . .

Somewhere outside a car backfires, and Saladin jolts. He is jarred now as the earth is jarred by the random shifts of plates. Inside him the world of then, with its dreams and boyhood and shame, merges with the world of now, where the hunger has returned to shred his stomach and the sun is hot and a kind old man is crazy enough to mumble at the floor. Saladin's whole body quivers and then shakes, a catastrophe of time and space, and he cannot stand still. He takes a candy bar off the shelf in front of the register, walks out of the gas station office and disappears down the busy boulevard. A few minutes later the manager will surface with a capless ballpoint pen.

Damn Arabs. Even when you try and help them . . . shit, you can't help anyone in this damn country.

And turns off the television.

Saladin moves through an afternoon of orange light, sweet hued and ill, that covers the city. He does not look for the ocean or avoid it, does not crave Hollywood or detest it, for all direction is meaningless now in this world that folds on top of itself, buckles beneath and crashes together so that every moment of one place is pushed atop every moment of another place until there is no chance for an exodus and no need to welcome the arrived.

★ ★ ★

Evening and the wind blows cool and soft, into the basin that holds the city and its thousand taquerias and rotisseries and dumpling houses and hamburger stands. The more Saladin walks through their aromas, the more he understands his hunger is a furious weakling, wanting and wanting but without muscle or means.

When he can no longer resist, he forgets about his faulty control of English and his lack of skills and walks into businesses at random. At an Armenian restaurant the smell of garlic and onions makes him mute and he forgets to answer the server, who speaks a poor Farsi heavily accented with Armenian vowels.

Hello. Can I help you?

He waits at Saladin's side for an answer, but Saladin can only take in the smell in deep, long breaths as if vapors alone could sustain him. From the back the voice of a woman shouts something hard and sharp and then *Irani!* and the waiter escorts Saladin out with a gentle hand to the elbow.

At a Korean salon a roomful of women giggle at his *Hello. Work. Today? I can work.* One of them takes his hand and smiles broadly.

Yes. We work today. Come here. I work for you.

Her smile is girlish but her teeth are dark and piled, and Saladin shakes himself free and leaves without apology or excuse.

Like this, he goes down the street. Into and out of businesses that ignore him or mock his clothes or hold their nose to his smell or entertain his query and desperation as long as it serves them.

Well, now. You say you are in what line of work?

We have use for only mechanics but you gotta be able to fix a Japanese car.

Maybe you could work in dry cleaning? Start with you own self.

By night he is in a neighborhood with more motorcycles than cars and men and women push against each other in phone booths and underneath neon-lit windows. From a dark doorway Saladin hears the familiar notes of the Rolling Stones song his brother tried to translate for him long ago. It is invitation enough and he goes in.

Except for two men on far stools the room is empty. The men, in black T-shirts and jeans and square-toed black boots, lean on a long wooden bar, a gathering of tiny glasses and beer bottles in front of them. One wears necklaces of beads and feathers and coins, and the other has his hair tied up behind him in a long ponytail. Behind the bar an old woman wipes down the taps and stares at Saladin but says nothing.

One of the men shouts.

You too, eh? You can't get no satisfaction either?

The men laugh and keep talking to him.

You might want to think about taking a shower. Girls don't much go for stinking Arabs.

Their words are loud and happy and said with a smile, and Saladin smiles in their direction and then in the direction of the bartender, who keeps narrow her old eyes.

Hello.

The bartender says nothing.

Work? I need work. I am a professional.

The bartender is a thin woman and her face falls around its

bones. She takes a long, last glance at him as if to make sure of something, then asks.

Where are you from?

My name is Saladin. Of the Ayyubids. Named for the great enemy to Richard the Lionheart . . .

He realizes he is speaking Farsi and quickly switches.

I will wash the dish. Work?

He gestures his hand to the area behind the bar.

Clean? I can—

I don't care what your name is. I know what you are, thought it the minute you walked in. You see that sign behind me?

None of the muscles in her face move when she speaks. She raises a bangled, freckled arm and points to a sign above the liquor bottles.

You probably can't read. Here, honey, let me help you. The sign says NO EYE-RAINIANS. Right there, and right under it says NO DOGS.

The men at the end start to laugh and shout down the bar at Saladin.

Come on now, Mary. You could be nicer to your guest. Come down here, man, let us buy you a beer.

Saladin is not sure what is being offered, but he walks down to them and stands at the bar as a beer is poured and placed in front of him by the old woman, who chuckles under her breath and shakes her head.

You two are terrible.

The men raise their empty glasses to him and Saladin does as he has seen it done in the movies, and they make the sound but only Saladin drinks, and on the craving stomach he is drunk after half a glass, and the one with the long hair and beaded necklaces has an arm around his shoulder and is asking questions Saladin cannot keep up with.

What business do you have taking our boys hostage?

Now you know you can't just fuck with Americans like that. You know why? Because we are patriotic, and that means that we are going to go over to your Iran and bomb the hell out of it to show you who's hostage. Don't you think so, Petey?

Then they are on both sides of him in an almost embrace. With every question they move a step closer.

Do your women have to wear those sheets because they are so fucking ugly no one wants to look at them?

When there are no more steps, they move a centimeter closer until Saladin feels like an animal before an attack, feeble and stuck. The aggression comes off their skin in waves, and they talk back and forth and through him as he tries to push back his stool and make for the door, but finds himself in the same position, not at all different from the position before, as if the idea to move was just that, an idea, as inconsequential as a daydream, and that all of his travel across mountains and barren deserts and cities and oceans and sky was to place him on this exact barstool to receive the bruises of knuckles that blow into his temples and gut. The force of one punch spins the lights and turns the music off, and again Saladin thinks to pick himself up off the floor and push them away and find the door to the outside, where he is innocent of whatever crime these men are punishing him for.

Nothing comes of the plan except a thick kick to his kidney and another to the small of his back, where pain and then a clear memory blooms: three older boys, brothers too, from a family that lived deep in the mountains and did not send their children to school. An afternoon at the end of fall, bare trees and clean air with a hard, cold edge. They watch him leave the cinema and cross the town square, and Saladin can sense them close behind, their steps nearer as he begins to walk the long stretch of emptiness before home. After a time they are beside him with insults so soft they are whispered in his ears: *Your maman was a Tehrani, and a whore in love with the Shah . . . What good is she here? Your baba is a traitor to all Kurds. What does that make you?* Saladin walks faster and thinks of Ali and of the chance they would have if he were here, and just as a foot trips him, just as he is on the ground kicking to try to keep the grabs and fists off, Ali is there, bigger than the oldest, strongest and more angry than any of them, and Saladin is up now, fighting alongside his brother, taking and giving and taking pain as well as they can, and for every time he falls or takes a hit, Saladin finds Ali in the mix and pushes himself up and forward until they are all hurt and the three boys from the mountains are cursing and walking away.

Tonight there is no brother, and one of the men has to pick Saladin up and drag him out to the sidewalk, while the other skips behind and tries to land another kick. His friend moves too fast and the boot misses and hits the leg of a chair, the side of the jukebox, Saladin's shoes. On the sidewalk there are curses before and after the final toss.

If we ever see you again . . . Go back to your desert . . . fucking immigrant . . .

The street moves past him, men and women and cars and

motorcycles, and when the desire to move comes, it is not from his head but from some momentary forgiveness of his body that lets him lift his legs and use his arms for balance against the walls of buildings, the stems of telephone poles and the backs of bus stop benches, and soon he is doing something like walking. A little blood is on his face, with a rip in the knee of his pants. Each step leads to another, and after a few hours his body cradles a deep soreness, but it moves and it is easier to keep on than it is to stand still, to remain. The streets of each neighborhood change, but the stares—curious, frightened, pitying—are all the same. He uses the sound of his heels to keep straight each tack and even to remind him he is, in fact, still in motion.

When the small sound disappears for a dozen or so strides, he looks down, and where there should be sidewalk there are rugs, four or five laid out on display, end to end, before an enormous plate-glass window that reads FARHANG MAHMOUDI. ORIENTAL RUGS, in Farsi and English. The patterns are warm and complex and old, just as he remembers them, and it is the same with the rugs as with the television news, and instantly the world of *there* is *here*. Exhausted, Saladin does not resist the overlap, does not try to ignore or erase this mess of time and space and self and walks into the rug store without a smile or a hello.

The rug seller sees him enter. There is the short look at the presence of a stranger, then the long look of recognition, and for both his face keeps the same expression. The merchant does not flinch at the sight of the blood or the bruises. He does not recoil at the scents of sweat and gasoline and mania but, always the professional, steps forward to greet his guest.

Salaam. Befaymin.

With an upturned palm that sweeps the air in toward the shop, he goes on.

Please, please, come in. Let us close the door behind you. We must be careful to keep the street out. Things are very dangerous these days. Come, my son. Come sit and I will fix you a cup of tea.

BELIEVERS

THE TWENTY-FOUR-YEAR-OLD WOMAN was a believer. She wore the copious black chador long before law mandated it and prayed reverently at every muezzin call. Like all true believers, she believed blindly, and when it was time, she clutched the heavy, rusted bolt cutter under her robes and followed instructions without a moment of hesitation.

Walk to the front gates of the embassy like you are a simple citizen. You will see they are bound together by a chain. Cut the chain. We will follow close behind you and storm the compound. Stay out of the way.

And so it goes.

Because a twenty-four-year-old woman believed deeply, blindly, our first years in this country were difficult. Just as our new life in America began to open for us, this woman and her act cast our days under a thick and heavy shade.

But that is only one way to consider it.

Some say forget it. Leave the girl alone. She was not the only woman willing to do it. Under the right circumstance, I might have. The Americans have been stealing our resources for years, and what did we do? Nothing. We envied their money and fashion, but none of it came to us. On the right day, I might have gone to the embassy myself.

If not her, they would have found someone else to cut the bolt. Khomeini and his men were going to take those hostages one way or another. She is irrelevant. There are thousands just like her.

Regardless of what they say, history will forget her name and the names of the men who stormed the embassy after her with guns and determination enough to yell threats and tie hands. History will remember the names of the hostages, their number (52) and the days of their captivity (444). History will note Khomeini's slithery negotiations, a failed rescue attempt involving a crashed helicopter and eight dead American servicemen. And history will make special mention of President Carter's ineptitude and President Reagan's heroism. A proud homecoming will mark all the books.

In the history of the Iranians it will be hard to forget the date, the act. November 4, 1979, a twenty-four-year-old woman, who goes nameless through time, sister of ours, performs a deed we suffer for, nine thousand miles away. Whether her deed was one of bravery or foolishness we cannot agree, but no one doubts that strong beliefs can be a dangerous thing.

As with everything else, there were good days and bad days. One minute we were filling out applications to work at a men's clothing store, the next minute the manager saw our names and started his shouts of *Get out of my store* and *You fucking Eyranian. I can't stand to look at one of you bastards!* And the minute after that we were walking out the door with our hearts in our throats. It was bad, yes, but at least it was noisy and honest, and the terrible stink of it only followed a soul around for so long. It was worse when our wives went to the grocer and the butcher where an angry man who watched the news on a tiny television knew enough about the crisis and the *crazy Muslims in Iran* to sell them only old cuts of pork.

I kept on pointing to the steak, to the roast, to the discounted ground beef, and he kept telling me, Today we only sell pork. Pig. You people can eat that, can't you? He would not even sell me a chicken back!

Between the good days and the bad, life kept on. What other option was there? We could not leave, even if we wanted to. Where would we go? We woke and slept and woke and slept and kept a brave face to one another and for our children and tried not to collapse every time we were alone on the streets, in the stores, on the highways, under the dark gazes.

For every kindness there was a terror. For each time a person asked *Where are you from?* and we answered honestly and the warmness stayed at the edges of their lips, there were times when our answer resulted in a withdrawn hand, narrowed eyes and a cold turn of the head. After a while we could not predict the reaction, and some of us failed ourselves and took to lying when asked.

Italian.

French.

Greek.

Spanish, from Spain, you know Madrid? Barcelona? It is a very beautiful country, yes. You should visit.

We were never entirely certain if the lie worked, but we convinced ourselves that it did and kept to it. For this, some of us felt more American, while the rest of us felt filthy. Our dark hair, our stature, the strong features of our face and our fashions identified, isolated and accused us. Our bodies became cages from which, lie or not, we could not escape. Some women dyed their hair blond. Some men changed their names to Jon or David or Ronny. The weaker among us refused Iranian friends, music, food. The bolder answered *Persian* to all questions and offered no explanation beyond that. In our own ways we all treaded lightly.

We waited it out and tried not answering at all, and when that was too much, we took to laughing. What else could we do? At night we sat in front of the evening news and watched the reports from coliseums and arenas full of men, black and white, upset with us and happy with themselves, in T-shirts that announced FUCK IRAN. We laughed at their painted signs of Khomeini with his turban on fire and their burning of the ancient flag and the banners that read *FREE THE HOSTAGES OR ELSE!* And *BOMB IRAN!* We shouted at the screen, *Go ahead!* and watched as grown men gathered and bonded over their hatred of us. They chanted and drank and stuffed their faces with peanuts and cotton candy and popcorn like boys at a circus, and all we could do was laugh.

We laughed, yes, but during those 444 days the suspicion leaked like a stain into the fabric of our new life. We could not even keep our children clean. They came home from schools where teachers refused to pronounce their names and students ignored them or poked fun at their accents, and they would stand before us and declare they hated school. We pleaded, *But maman jaan, tomorrow will be different. I promise.* We lied. We knew nothing about tomorrow for them or for ourselves and could not predict when our colleagues—the other doctors, or workmen, or business associates—would throw us a greasy look, deny us a position or promotion, claim our English was insufficient, or that our educations, work ethics, presence, were somehow *lacking.*

The crisis dragged on. For months the hostage takers made their one demand: *The Shah. Give us the Shah.* On day 216 the Shah died, and though only a few of us were sad, all of us asked.

What will they ask for now? What offering will bring this to an end?

All around us trees were tied with yellow ribbons, and every day some new negotiation was in the news. Khomeini demands twenty million for the safe release of the fifty-two Americans held hostage in Tehran. Khomeini demands twelve million for the safe release of the fifty-two Americans held hostage in Tehran. In a new bid to negotiate Khomeini has asked the United States for eight million to ensure the safe release of the fifty-two Americans held, in poor conditions, in the former U.S. embassy in Tehran. There are reports they have resorted to drinking boiled water from the pool.

And still the dark gazes followed us wherever we went. At red lights we sat, stuck, behind cars with bumper stickers that said GET RID OF THE TOWEL HEADS, and we thought to ourselves, *We came for this?* When we took our Sunday strolls on the Santa Monica pier and the American families moved out of our way, far to the other side of the pier, we asked, *We came for this?* When the police answered our calls about harassment they too asked.

Well, what did you come here for? The great American dream? Paradise?

During this period we had no answers. All we knew was that we had left an ugly time behind and had somehow arrived in an ugly time, and the girl forgotten by history walked about our dreams with her bolt cutters and mysterious, determined smile. One of thousands.

On the day the movie star became president, the fifty-two hostages were released. We asked each other, *Isn't that president familiar? I think he is the actor. Yes! The actor, from that old film, the one with the monkey* . . . We wondered at the timing, but said nothing, so great was our relief. When it was revealed that the hostages were exchanged for arms that went directly to the revolutionary guards, who sold them directly to South America to fuel yet another story of bloody revolution and sorrow in a country most of us had never heard of, we did not care. The scandal was not our business, and we breathed a collective sigh, an inhale and exhale, our first truly American breath, as we had now survived this trial on this soil and so perhaps we had, in some way, earned our stay. Around us the Americans continued to cast their dark glances for some time afterward, like a car with bad brakes coming to a stop. They said little to us in those days and finally said nothing at all, not even hello. For a time we did the same.

We took solace in one another and then in this place with its beautiful gardens and wide beaches and small pockets of paradise. Some of us rejuvenated as we hiked the hills of Griffith Park, where we walked slowly beneath the fragrant shade of the tall eucalyptus groves.

Such elegant trees.

We have nothing like this in Iran.

A century ago there was nothing like this in America either. The *Eucalyptus globulus*, a nonnative species, was introduced to the coast in 1890 by an Australian scientist determined to show how their deep roots could stabilize the eroding California coastal soil. Botanists, nationalists, gardeners denied it, and the tall tree arrived to poor prospects. Scientists and park planners dismissed it, convinced the resident species—oak, madrone, pine—were better equipped against local predators and disease and it was only a matter of time before these new arrivals would be overrun. With little hope for their longevity the Australian botanist planted them anyway, loath to see the seeds and saplings go to waste after surviving the cross-Pacific journey.

The predictions fell short, turned out to be unfounded and untrue. The root systems did nothing to stabilize the soil or provide nutrients to the sandy shale, but the trees took heartily to the slopes and piedmonts up and down California and thrived far longer than any nay-saying American expert could have expected. Before long the coast was spotted with patches of eucalyptus groves. After the hostage crisis some of us walked through those high cathedrals of soft, peeling bark and took our time to breathe in the spicy smell of their fresh perfume, stretch our shoulders and necks and heads to let the sparkling shadows of their slender leaves dance over our upturned faces.

IN THE COMPANY OF MEN

THE OCEAN IS warm, and except for a group of children swimming nearby, Saladin is alone in it. The water stings his tender cuts, but after a few strokes away from shore the weightlessness feels good and he swims farther out, where he treads water and watches a group of thin, gray fins bob up and down. He stares and does not know sharks or dolphins or the difference between the two and watches them swim near and then away and wonders what other life fills this deep into which he cannot see.

Near the shore a boy from the group of children floats on his back, toes pointed up, eyes closed. His face is as calm as the sky it mirrors, and Saladin copies him and the sea easily holds him up, and for a time he feels nothing, not pain or worry or confusion or the small sorrow that sobbed in him on the walk home last night when the wounds pierced with such intensity he could not even cry. The boy rights himself in the water and swims over.

I'll race you in.

His eyes are the color of water close to the shore. Saladin nods.

Yeah? Ready? Set! One. Two. Three.

The boy's body splashes away and Saladin follows behind as quickly as he can, and where the waves start, he treads water and watches the boy lay his body as flat and stiff as a board and glide in on the crest of a wave. Saladin copies him, and like that the ocean pushes him gently to shore. He takes it as an omen, on this fourth day. He dresses in a way that doesn't hurt and checks to make sure the rug seller's few dollars are still in his pocket.

There is also a note, in formal script, and Saladin reads it and remembers how the rug seller read it to him twice and then explained once more.

Listen carefully, just in case you get lost. You catch the bus here. This number. The bus driver will go a long way, and then he will call Westwood. Just like that. Westwood! And then you get off.

Saladin waits at a sign for the bus that matches the numbers on his note. When the door opens, he puts all his change in a small box beside the steering wheel and waits for the driver to give him permission to board, to say, *That is enough, please, come along*. But the driver does not move and the bus does not move and behind Saladin a Chinese woman pushes his hip with her tiny hand. Saladin takes his place in a long row of seats at the back, near the window where more than anything else he would like to look out at the Los Angeles that he moves through by motor for the first time, but is continually distracted by a man in black glasses and a fur hat who speaks without stop.

Every time Saladin turns to look out the window, the man pokes him in the arm with a stiff finger and demands.

Hey, man. Heeeey, maaaan. I am talking to you.

At the contact Saladin cannot help but tense and think of the men from the bar. He moves his body as close to the window as he can, and the fur hat, a creature unto itself, leans toward him like a hungry animal.

Brother, what are you afraid of? I'm not gonna hurt you.

His clothes are appropriate for the snow, and the soles of his shoes flap at great distance from his toes.

Now you see, the Constitution says that we are all allowed this and that. But that is not equal, is it? What we really need to chew on is the Declaration of Independence, right, brother? Now, let me tell you this. It tells us. All. Men. Are. Created. Equal. You believe that, brother? I tell you, some days . . . some days . . .

The man takes a feather buried deep inside his shirt and waves it slowly in front of his nose as if to hypnotize himself.

Now you. Are you equal to me?

Saladin watches him and thinks how he will answer a question he does not understand.

I am Saladin. Nice to meet you.

The man offers his hand and the two engage in an awkward side-to-side handshake. In front of them a younger man wears a thin white mask over his mouth and, with eyes closed, touches everything around him as if he were blind. When he has felt the bus, the window, his shins and hair, he pretends to play a piano that rests invisibly atop his bare knees. After a time the bus fills with mothers and grandmothers and men in blue and white work shirts, and everyone but the children are tired through the eyes and the face. Saladin catches the gaze of a toddler, who smiles at him instantly and without reluctance. Every now and again the tan-skinned man stabs Saladin's shoulder and he no longer flinches at the touch but wonders how it is that all these people, not bound by history or tribe or even appearance, do not kill each other a little bit every day.

The ride is long. The city is enormous and does not seem to end in any direction. He remembers the vista from the tall building and knows as long as the bus is moving toward the mountains, it is the right direction. At some point the fur-hat man leans down to gather his bags and prepares to disembark. He stands before Saladin with all of his belongings and necklaces, and as the bus stops, he embraces Saladin's head into his crotch in a furious hug that smells like semen and shit.

That's it, brother. We got to keep the love alive. Remember. Forget everything I told you. God be with you, my brother. We all need him.

The man laughs loud and wide and the rest of the bus stares as if he were an affliction on them all. Without him the bus is empty and dull and Saladin looks out the window at the thin crowds that spot the streets and sidewalks and imagines that he sees himself walking down this boulevard: a man on the way to work, behind him a warm bed and blue-eyed woman still asleep. His street self has the same dark hair, but it is combed and washed and smells of cologne. He wears a gray suit and his briefcase and sunglasses and leather wallet are all top-of-the-line. From the window Saladin watches this imagined self walk hurriedly from one good fortune to the next, so busy and glad he does not stop for one second to look up and consider the unwieldy bus or the passenger he once was.

* * *

When he arrives, the rug seller insists on tea and stares at the wounds on Saladin's face and hands, but mentions nothing. When they have dissolved two sugar cubes each and emptied the samovar, they go to a small warehouse behind the store, and the merchant instructs Saladin in a tone more conversational than commanding.

Sometimes you might want to vacuum the rugs. If you do, please put them over there.

He points to a pile in the middle of the room.

And maybe sometimes you want to hit them with the end of a broom like your maman did. Then it would be good if you laid them out and stacked them flat over there.

He points to a corner of the warehouse.

Sometimes you want to ship them, and those go over there. And then there are some for display and . . . just try and keep things jam o jour back here.

Jam o jour. Together and ordered. His mother used that expression to describe how she liked the pantry, her closet and drawers, the children's school supplies. It is the mark of an order Saladin has long lost in his life, and he lets the memory of it, the possibility of it, resonate a moment. The rug seller looks at him.

Yes. Of course. Jam o jour. Of course.

The rugs are dusty, of varied ages and in various conditions, but all of them are sold as new. Saladin knows better, and in the day spent cleaning and rolling and stacking, he thinks about the years of their making. The years the ewe had to live before its first wool could be shorn or the length of the worm's life before it would unspin its silk. There are the years it took the plant to grow the flower that makes the dye, and the years of the girls and boys who knotted and knotted and knotted as years passed, and even the years of the patternmaker, who might have spent a lifetime receiving designs from the divine so that here in America the rugs can be sold as if they were pressed out from a machine just yesterday. Saladin tries to remember to ask the rug seller why this is, why he must lie, but forgets to mention it until it becomes normal, the way of things.

At the end of the day the rug seller hands him a small stack of bills and another piece of notebook paper.

Please forgive me if I intrude. I don't know your situation, but if your family is not here yet . . . and you have no place . . . you can take a room at the house of this man. He is a good man. Mexiki, but clean, and his price is not bad. He sells clothes too, razors, soap and things. Ask for Agha Calderon. Tell him Farhang from Westwood sent you.

The rug seller returns to his ledgers. Saladin pretends that it is unnecessary but takes the note and the money, even though he knows a conversation like this between men is shameful. It is shameful not to have a family that takes care of you, shameful not to have a home, to be in a situation, to have a swollen face you cannot, will not, explain. It does not matter now. The note, the first day's pay, the possibility of a bed, in Los Angeles, California, America, this matters now. Saladin offers his one hand, and the rug seller takes it between the both of his and holds on.

It is my pleasure, my son. We will find our way. Truly.

Calderon cooks and talks and cooks and moves about the kitchen with an ease Saladin has only ever seen in women. An apron hangs to his ankles, and for no evident reason he wears soccer cleats. An old Tabriz carpet is in the kitchen, and from the oven and off the stove smells burst forth that make the kitchen a strange place, intoxicating and chaotic, and Saladin sits and listens patiently to some long story that might, or might not, end in food.

Me? I came eleven years ago in the backseat of a car full of soldiers. I paid American army boys one hundred dollars to take me across the border. First they put me in the trunk, but it didn't work. I couldn't do it, like a criminal or a dead person, and I hit the door of the trunk until they let me out. I was sure they were going to leave me on the side of the highway, but one of them, a black, took off his army jacket and put it on my shoulders. Say nothing, he told me. That's how I left Tijuana, and that is how I came to California. Smelling like pussy and sweat and cheap beer. Heh. I had some money. I had a gold cross from my mother and a note, like the note your *jefe* gave you, from my brother, who came first.

Meat sizzles in a pan, and the oil reaches back down to the burner and makes for a bigger flame. Saladin does not even think about a fire, so controlled is the man in his actions and intentions.

I had a note too, just like yours. My brother told me, he said, go to this address, if the fence is open, walk around to the back and take the steps all the way up. When there are no more steps, you will see a ladder to the roof. Tell whoever is there that you are my brother, and then sleep, *hermano*, sleep, and I will come find you.

I remember it just like it was yesterday. You will remember these days too. For some reason they stay fresh in the mind. There were five of us up there. It was no more than a chicken coop with walls made of tin, and the ceiling was made of a wavy sheet of green plastic, and when the light came in, it made all of us look sick. The floor had mattresses all over it, and I can still remember some of them had sheets with cartoon characters on them that I watched as a boy, in Mexico. Mickey Mouse. Donald Duck. The redheaded woodpecker.

It was hot all the time. There were a few things, a camping stove, dishes, an orange cooler we tried to keep full of water. Sometimes, if it was early in the month, we kept some groceries—tortillas, cheese, beans—nothing fancy, nothing like this, nothing cooked. I think there was a TV too, maybe it was broken . . . We used to tape the plug of our radio down the side wall of the building all the way into old Garciela's window. That *viejita*. She lived alone with her candles and saints and other Cristo garbage and charged us five cents every time we wanted to use her bathroom, ten cents for a shower and twenty if we wanted hot water. Her door was always open, but I can't say I ever said a nice thing to her. She liked me too. Always called me *hijo* and turned on the heat without saying anything. I was good-looking too. Like you. Skinny too, like you. But still my life was hard and I lived on that rooftop for two years.

But you know. Time passes. You will see how fast as soon as you make your way. Now eleven years. I bought this house as soon as I could, saved every penny from the job I had planting and sweeping and mowing at the Beverly Hills golf club. You ever played golf, *hermano*? Such a boring game. Every cent I kept for this place, and when I got it, my brother and I tore down those walls and put up these, and now it sleeps fifteen when it's full. I made the bunks myself. Who is to say just because you are new to this country you have to live in a shitty basement, or on a hot roof? Not me, *hombre*.

Come. Stay here. You have a room this week, my food is good, your *jefe* is good, America is okay, maybe it will get better. You can do whatever you want with it.

The smell of pork fills the kitchen, and Saladin's stomach turns in hunger at the scent of this novel meat. He cannot believe how much the man has talked and realizes it has been a long time since he has been in a home where men are comfortable, relaxed enough to tell a story. Calderon looks at him, and whatever it is he sees in Saladin makes him put his spatula down and take off the overlong apron.

Vamanos. Let me show you your bed. All the men feel better when they see the place they will sleep.

The room is small and full of beds stacked in pairs on tall wooden frames. Out one window there is a cracked cement yard with a few overturned milk crates and an empty cooler. In a nearby yard Saladin can hear a dog bark, whimper and then bark again, and though the sound is near, the dog is nowhere to be seen. Saladin does not move about the room, does not take his hands out of his pockets. Calderon hits a mattress on a bottom bunk and a cloud of dust fills the air.

For you. Warm. Comfortable. Clean. Seven other men sleep here.

Calderon laughs.

Well, my friend, what were you expecting? Pink champagne on ice? I have only ever seen pink champagne in the movies. Here we have only the most delicious beer.

Calderon extends his hand. Saladin pushes forth his own hand for a series of firm shakes that speak a gratitude he does not, at the moment, feel.

Thank you. Yes. It is very nice. Very very beautiful. Thank you.

And Calderon nods and nods again and smiles and is glad with himself and his new guest and repeats over and over.

You will be fine here. You have made it this far, rest before we eat, take a rest before the other men come . . .

In a habit he will keep for most of his life, Saladin takes off his shoes and places them beside the door. Sand leaks out and he leaves behind small prints of dirt and sweat as he moves from bed to bed to look at the shirts and hats and carefully folded pants. On the walls beside pillows are magazine pullouts of women, photographs of children, drawings and small maps of countries he has never heard of: Guatemala, Honduras, Mexico. In the largest space of wall there is a map of Colombia, all of the main cities burned through with perfect holes. Saladin tucks himself into the bottom bunk, and without his trying his muscles relax and his bones sink. The plywood of the bunk above him is close, but not as close as the wood slats of the pier, and he closes his eyes and hears the dog in the near yard whimper and bark, whimper and bark. When he wakes, the boarding room is full of men in various stages of undress. They come and go from the shower, the bathroom, the telephone that rings and slams against the hallway wall. Now the smell of fried meat is everywhere, and when Saladin sits up, he knocks his head on the bottom of the bunk, and one of the men smiles at him warmly and repeats words in a language that make no sense.

Cuidate, hermano, cuidate.

HOW TO MAKE A HOME

LAY THE BODY down on the bed.

Sleep through darkness into day.

At first this will be enough.

If you have belongings, personal effects, unpack them, but do not put them away in drawers or cabinets or closets with any immediacy. Let them sit out for an hour, a few days, so they can greet you when you enter a room and you can catch sight of that sweater your grandmother knit and you can relax, remember, remind yourself, Yes. This is where I live. This is my room. Look! There are my socks!

Relax on the toilet, take longer than necessary. Relax in the shower. Stand naked in the bathroom with the door closed until you are dry. If you have the house to yourself for some time, stand naked in as many rooms as you can. Let the house, which is getting to know you as well as you are getting to know it, see you as you are. Walk down the hallways, sit on the cold floors and pose precariously close to the windows. Dress when you are comfortable with yourself.

Notice the threshold every time you step over it.

Lie down on the kitchen floor.

Let things find their places. The shampoo and the soap, the small pile of shoes at the door, the butter, the spoons, the trash and the hook for the keys. Study the views from the windows. See the street, the small palm, the neighbor's grill, wait for the cat that sometimes comes and goes from the grassy patch just outside the bedroom that you can't get to. Study the views that have nothing to do with windows, the sights you will, without wanting or trying, see every day: the ceiling above your pillow, your face in the bathroom mirror, the mark on the wall of the living room that looks like a letter in a language you are still learning.

Decorate.

Sew curtains or buy elaborate blinds. Draw them down, darken a room, keep out the world you don't yet understand. When you can, stay inside, gather yourself, hold still for as long as it takes for the calm to cover you.

Buy a thick comforter that will keep you warm regardless of the temperature. Hang pictures. If you can bear it, hang photographs of so-and-so and so-and-so. If you can't bear it, leave the wall empty until new photographs are made of you smiling in the new *here* and the new *there*.

Cook a rich meal, richer than necessary, of meat stew and a side of fresh greens—onions, basil, mint and radish—eat the living and the dead in your new home. Relish.

Take a long midday nap.

Buy a plant. Cut a limb from it and replant it in another pot. Let the severed bit grow.

Yes, you will complain there is no garden and there is no fountain and no grandfather's smoking bench and no grandfather. The balcony will have to suffice. Turn it into a paradise of jasmine and honeysuckle and impatiens, a lifted Eden of seeds you planted and watered; a collection of life that exists because of and for you alone.

And, no. No uncle and no aunt and no favorite cousin will eat at your table or grace your living room with their old silly jokes, take tea with you and nod as you worry and explain this or that passing trouble. Stay still. This is your home now. They will come.

Find your way to the bedroom.

Lay the body down on the bed.

Let them visit you in dreams.

FLY-FLY

THE BOARDINGHOUSE IS full of maps, and on his first morning Saladin walks from one to the next and looks at the shapes of countries, the great waters, the way Los Angeles hangs off America. He knows he has to be at work soon, he knows too that the rug seller will not be upset with him if he is late.

The last time Saladin studied a map was on the island. There were a few small ones and one large one, almost entirely blue with only a few specks of land. They were taped up to the wall of the airplane hangar, and Saladin and Ali stood before them as the mechanic explained their location by circling around a small green dot with his oily fingernail and repeating the fact of the island to them, again and again.

Ilha. Azores. Ilha dos Azores.

The man seemed to be carved of copper. His eyes, his hands and face, the skin of his arms and even his tight, curly hair were a deep shade of orange.

The man shook his head and started again with the finger and the circles and the slow words.

Ilha. Azores. Eu.

He pointed to himself and nodded yes vigorously.

Sí. Me.

He pointed to the brothers and the other men from the ship that gathered behind them.

No. Você. You. No no no no. Clandestino. Policía. Home. Go. Go. Ciao-ciao. O—

He gestured to the plane behind them.

Fly-fly.

To the men from the cargo ship, the island was an insult, a cruel joke, a curse. After the night of their near death they waited for the container to land on what felt like solid ground and immediately climbed up the ladder and out into a sunny world for which they had no name. Behind them there were docks and ships and endless water, and they moved away quickly, running down an asphalt road that turned to dust after the first few meters. They kept on it, and when people passed, Saladin thought to ask where was it they had come to and where they should go, but he did not know what language to speak, the people were so unfamiliar. Their skin was deep or medium or light brown, and they wore cheap, clean clothes and large straw hats. They did not raise their eyes to offer a greeting or even recognize this flock that smelled of vomit and piss and fear. The children that passed all stared at the men, and a few of the infants let out long, shrill wails.

They walked one kilometer, maybe two, and Saladin felt panic start to pass among them. The men muttered to themselves and shouted at each other in English and other languages.

Where is this? What shit have I eaten to end up here?

Saladin looked at Ali beside him, and Ali looked around him like a tourist in the movies, hands in pockets, carefree, as if it made no difference that they survived or that they might be lost or that his younger brother, responsible for this mess, wanted some reassurance.

Ali. Do you know where this is?

Ali looked away, up at the sun and down at his shadow, and pretended he did not hear.

A small Datsun truck pulled up behind their slow-moving group, and a man leaned his head out the window and asked, Turkey? Iran? Afghanistan?

Saladin and the Turkish twins and a few others ran to the open window and shouted, *Yesyesyes*.

The man was pale with dark black curls and he instructed them in a slow English. Follow me. Follow behind the truck.

He drove in front and led them down a dirt path and then another and then down a road of soft green grass to a clearing with a long, cracked cement runway and an airplane hangar with no door.

The men followed the truck to a river, where the driver waited while they stripped off their clothes and washed. Saladin had never seen such trees before, sky-high, with enormous leaves and ropy branches that netted together at the top. Everywhere he looked the green canopies twinkled with tiny white and red and yellow birds, and all around his feet insects with black and green and red speckled backs jumped about. Ali didn't seem to notice any of it and joined the others as they washed their bodies and then their clothes and then spread out naked on the hot rocks and slept. When Saladin tried to swim, the pain was too great and he looked down to find his body covered in the bruises and dark green welts of someone who had been trampled in some great exodus. He looked at the bodies of the other men, of his brother, and but for their hair and size and age, the damage to their bodies was sometimes more and sometimes less.

The driver took them to the hangar, where they found a few tables and chairs, a dozen or more small metal cots, tools, engine parts, and empty barrels of oil. There were two unmatched propellers and a large, rusted plane without seats or windows or wings that seemed, aside from its condition, as if it could carry a hundred men into the sky. The gathered men stood in front of the broken machine and thanked their gods. Their shoulders dropped and one or two of them even smiled.

The driver leaned out the window of his truck and spoke.

They come in the morning. One every morning. For a price. A cost. Sometimes America, sometimes England. Maybe Canada. Talk with the pilots. They have a price for you. Bem.

Those who could left quickly. They produced secreted chains of gold, Swiss watches, cuff links, paper money, and agreed upon a distance that matched the value of their offerings. Saladin sat on the grass beside the runway and watched the windowless beasts peel themselves off the ground by what seemed like the force of sound alone. The wind from their takeoff soothed him, and every time they launched, a little part of his insides lifted too, just as he had planned. He had watched that lift in birds since he was a boy, the way the wind took them just beneath the wings, the way, if they let it, the wind did all the work. In his life of wanting—to leave the mountain town; to walk into the world of the screen; to be an American and live out the life of a new hero with an old name—he never wanted anything more than a place on these planes with their cool and clean getaway.

When the men from Saladin's boatload had paid and flown, other men came, from other boatloads, still covered in a thin film of horror from the night or nights just passed. They found places to sit and sleep, and those who could not stood studiously before the mechanic who circled the tiny green dot on the map and pronounced again and again.

ILHA. I-L-H-A. Azores.

The mechanic would go on to explain, in some mix of English and other tongues Saladin had never heard, that they could not stay. The island was full of *policía* who made sure no men were on boats or planes. They searched the hangars and the docks with, the mechanic made the shape with his greasy hand, *pistolas*, and they sent each man back to his first home. After a few days Saladin and Ali were the only men left, and no matter how Saladin searched himself and his brother, he could not find an item of value between them. They listened to the mechanic talk and ate the food left by the boy who cooked for the pilots and took turns sleeping on the blanket they shared. New men came and went, the mechanic warned them all of *pistolas* and *policía* and the hangar held and let go of their lives as easily as it kept and released the fragrant island wind.

On the third day Ali, against the warnings of the mechanic, left the hangar. Saladin ran to catch him.

Where are you going?

For a walk.

For what?

For nothing. Just a walk. I told you, it relaxes me.

The island, with its mud streets and barefoot children, held no interest for Saladin. It had the same quiet dullness of the mountain town, and he could not understand why his brother found comfort in places where everything had already happened and there was nothing new left to do. He knew Ali did not follow the dreams his mother had set out before them, but Saladin knew too that his brother was a man of ambition, ambition to honor what their father had stained, ambition to become a truer version of the old man. Why Ali could not find this honor in America bothered Saladin, and he dismissed his brother's moods and sarcasm as symptoms of some bigger confusion, some passing sickness born of the constant movement and uncertain direction of these last few days and weeks.

Saladin paced the hangar and focused his attention on the pilots who stayed in or near their planes, where the desperate refugees approached them with goods or promises or simple begging. The pilots spoke in English and sometimes in French, and once, from a pilot in the jacket of the Shah's air force, in Farsi. They always took the offering when the offering was good and rejected small sums, tarnished jewelry, useless trinkets. Regardless of what was given or how enormous the plane, the pilots refused to fly any more than three or four men at a time. Saladin eavesdropped on conversations, spoke with men who had been granted permission or denied and walked the floor of the hangar for days, hopeful and without despair.

Each night Ali's mood improved. He returned from his walks with handfuls of loamy dirt, seashells that held the sound of the ocean, colorful dead birds—all of which he laid out before Saladin, astonished at his own finds.

Can you believe this? We had nothing like it in the mountain town. Imagine Baba's face when he sees this painted bird, all of his pigeons were gray gray gray.

A fever shone in his brother's eyes and he was unable to look at anything—Saladin, the other men, the ceiling of the hangar—for too long. Saladin watched Ali's fast gestures and nervous blinks and said nothing when he erupted in nonsensical talk.

What do you think the plums in Agha Mostaffa's orchard will taste like this fall? Who do you think they missed more? Me or you? I can't wait to eat Khanoum Mitra's rice again. How long since we had good rice . . . ?

The island was hot and Ali's walks were long and Saladin suggested his brother drink a little more water.

Ali, soon we will be gone.

How do you know that, Saladin jaan? We cannot seem to go forward from here. It is best to start planning a way back, don't you think?

★ ★ ★

After a few days the brothers stopped speaking. They spent the mornings and afternoons apart and shared a space on the floor but no conversation. When the latest group of men arrived, with their rancid smell, slumped bodies and hollow, roving eyes, Ali left the hangar without more than one look. Even the mechanic kept his distance from this flock, which seemed to have strayed just out of death's reach. But Saladin kept close, watched them sleep on the cement floor and pointed them in the direction of the river when they woke. They bathed like specters, and Saladin learned all he needed to know from the gashes on their knees and blistered feet, the burn marks and long red signatures of rods or whips. Most of them were so dirty that even after they bathed their hair still stood on end. There were relations in this group, fathers and sons, cousins, brothers and what seemed like a few friends. When they returned to the hangar, they spread themselves out and slept again. A light-eyed father and his light-eyed son sat next to Saladin, and the father spoke to him in Farsi, as if it were the only language on earth.

Forgive us for taking up your space. We are tired. Very tired.

Please, sit. It is not my space.

Yes. Well.

The father sat down and crossed his legs, and his son, a boy of four or five, sat in between them and the four eyes looked up at Saladin.

What is ours anymore?

The son looked up at Saladin, and the father slowly began to take off his shoes. The leather was cracked at the bend near the toes, and one shoe had no heel.

The situation is bad. Most likely worse than when you left. We are all victims. Every last one of us, just barely alive enough to leave. Do you see that man there? Brother of the owner of the Golestan hotel, you know, the big one in Tehran ... A month after the revolution his brother was called out into the streets in front of the hotel and shot by the guardsmen, boys really. His crime? Giving rooms to British and Americans. And that man there? In the checkered shirt? A Jew, son of a jeweler, apparently an athlete of some fame. A wrestler or something. They raided his house in the Jewish neighborhood of Shiraz. The servant tried to protect his children, but the gendarmes shot him, in front of all his children. What is left of the family is in Karachi now. I don't know where he is going. I don't think he does either.

The man stopped and looked directly at Saladin.

Where are you going?

Amreeka. California. Hollywood. With my brother.

To family?

Yes. We are going to meet our uncle. He is waiting for us there.

Saladin did not pause before he spoke and the words came easily, like truth.

The man took the child up into his arms. The child's eyes were drowsy and a large red welt was on his forehead.

Good. Family. I think family is all we have. These days especially.

The father kissed his boy, rested his chin on his small head of brown hair and shut his own heavy eyes like a man who slept only when his son was quiet and dreaming, no more, no less.

That night a dream clutched Saladin with such ferocity that he woke in a sweat and without breath. He sat up in shock and could not, for some reason, stand the sight of his brother asleep next to him. He looked at the calm face, the neatly aligned bones, the handsome dimple in the chin, and saw in them their father and pieces of himself and the dream flickered back to life in his head. The jungle around them was filled with women. Grown women with the faces of girls jumped from branches and climbed up trunks and rested in the high leafy canopies. Saladin and his brother were old, much closer to death than to birth, and they still lived in the hangar and they still did not speak. Afraid to miss a plane, Saladin stood at the entry of the hangar, bent and weak boned and bald, and pleaded with the women, *Please, please come in.* The women refused him and waited for Ali, wrinkled and jaunty with a full head of hair, as he walked out into the jungle and took a nymph by the shoulders or waist as she pushed down his pants and took him inside her, and Saladin was left to watch and want this love he had never, in his dreams or life, had. He kicked his brother awake.

Ali. Ali!

Ali stretched luxuriously as if he had been having the same dream.

Wake up! Let's go for one of your walks.

What?

A walk. I want to go on the walk with you. You say it is a beautiful place. Show me. Wake up. Show me.

They walked out away from the runway and into the jungle on a steep, narrow mountain path. At every rustle Saladin searched for a woman but saw only small, hairless animals and a few birds. Beside him Ali moved slowly, stopping to pick up stones or flowers or examine the patterns on the backs of giant bugs.

This world is much bigger than I ever thought.

Ali remarked before a resting butterfly with pink-and-black wings.

All this life, together, at the same time. Our sisters back home are still combing their hair, maybe still crying for us. The foreman in Istanbul is still printing newspapers, the girl in Cagliari is with a million men tonight. Who knows . . . I thought all that ever happened in the world happened in the mountain town.

Ali never spoke like this, and Saladin let the dream fade and let himself listen to his brother.

I have been thinking about Babak.

Not once have they said his name. Saladin knew it when the men were lined up and knew it when Babak squirmed beneath him, still alive, blindfold falling off. He has known it all these walking days, but not once had either brother mentioned him, said the word out loud.

Sometimes I feel as if Babak is right beside us. Right here, Saladin jaan, in the space between me and you.

The butterfly flew in small graceful arcs around Ali's head, and at certain angles the sun shone through the wings to reveal intricate dusty patterns.

I can feel him, the ghost of him. It follows us everywhere, lost as we are lost. Sometimes I think it is because he is unburied. Because he is still on the valley floor and his spirit is restless.

Ali, what are you talking about? We have come too far . . . In Los Angeles . . .

We should go back. Bury him. Be with our people. Even Baba stayed. He could have lived his life as a traitor in Tehran or Esfahan, took a higher post even, less ridicule, but even he choose to come back to the town he was born in. What difference does it make that he came back in the uniform of the Shah? At least he stayed. Only the very truest cowards leave.

The blood rushed to Saladin's head and then cleared and left him with a precise clarity of thought.

If Baba had not come back to Kermanshah, if he had gone far away, to Mashhad or Qom or Tehran, we would not be in this mess! It would have made a big difference. You must think survival cowardly. If you can live in America, as a man, without a gun, does that mean you are a coward? If your son can live without fighting about blood, is that cowardly?

Ali put out his finger and the butterfly landed on it, pulsed with the rhythm of a running man come to rest.

There is always a way home.

Ali held the butterfly up between their faces.

It is just like Khanoum Alevi taught us in biology class, how the animals and insects migrate, away and back.

They came to a town of six or seven streets and walked through morning activities that carried on as if they weren't there. Women in sandals stirred large iron pots over fires, and men rested, half asleep, in slung beds of thin netting. Children ran to grab Ali's hand and held it and smiled up at him as if they already knew there was no common tongue between them and the tall, happy stranger. A man in a military uniform and white sash stood in the open window of what looked like a café. He drank slowly from a tiny ceramic cup, and when the brothers passed, he looked long at Saladin and nodded once to Ali. Ali met the glance and nodded back.

Do you want to see their water, their big ocean?

Ali asked. He was in a good mood, smiling at the faces they met and walking with an extra bend in his step. Once in a while he whistled a few notes from the Beatles song "Help!"

No. Ali, who was that man?

What man?

Just as Saladin started to ask why he knew a man in military uniform and why a man in military uniform knew him, a big-bellied airplane flew low over their heads in the direction of the hangar. Saladin forgot his question, his brother, the morning's frustrating talk, and started his run back.

Ali laughed behind him.

Hurry! Maybe it will land on your finger!

The Iranian air force pilot took no questions. He explained himself once slowly, and then again, and then no more.

If you have nothing to exchange for the trip, you will work for us, in our warehouse in Los Angeles, for two months per person. You will fly for the cost of your labor. If you are two, you will work for two months each, or four if you have an old man or a child. That is the cost of your trip. The work is easy and you will be excused after the two months. We can take you all. We leave at seven tomorrow morning.

The men's voices rose up in a flood of questions, and the pilot waited for the silence and repeated himself exactly, then walked up the sloped steps into the narrow, oval door. Saladin understood the man completely, and when Ali returned from his walk, Saladin acted as if nothing had changed.

How was the walk?

Beautiful. They have birds here that can whistle whole songs.

Yes?

And I ate a meal with a fried sweet banana in it. Saladin, you really should try—

Saladin could no longer refrain. The words and thoughts and dreams all came out in a calamitous, senseless rush.

After our two months I am going to take work anywhere I can. Well, not anywhere, not a gas station or anything with garbage. Maybe something to do with banks. Hosseini worked in a bank. What do you think factory work is like? Do you think we will be able to afford motorcycles or should we first buy a car to share? Easy I am sure. Ali, can you believe it? Can you believe we can finally go? Tomorrow they said, directly to Los Angeles, without stop?

Ali stared at him as if he were crazy.

What are you talking about?

Saladin had forgotten to mention the pilots, the plane, the negotiation of work. He laughed at himself.

That plane. The big one. The pilots will take us to Los Angeles. We have to work for them, factory work, for two months when we get there. That is the cost. But we don't need papers, passports. We don't need money.

And you believe them?

Yes. They said—

Ali sat down on his cot and spoke in a stern voice.

Saladin jaan, if this is true, then you go, but I will not come. It is not the way I am going.

Ali kicked off his shoes and stared at them on the ground.

The excitement had made Saladin unstable, and the thought of his brother's leaving him, of the journey going in two directions, riled him and he felt the hot water of tears streak his face. He had planned for America all his life, yes, but he had never planned a life without Ali. Even in his plans from before, Saladin had always imagined his brother would, after a time, join him, take his own place in the American dream. Now, just as America was a true possibility, as close and probable as the plane that rested behind them, Saladin understood that it could be otherwise, that there could be a future, in America, without brother and alone. He had begged of his brother before—for his help to build the pool, money for the cinema, to please leave Van, Istanbul, to keep going—and there was no pride to stop him from doing it again.

Saladin knelt and found his brother's eyes.

You would go back without me? Let me go on the plane alone?

Ali met Saladin's stare and made no gesture of yes, no gesture of no.

There is work, Ali. We can get an apartment. Girlfriends . . . Maman would be proud of us. She told me it is what she wanted most, for her children to live their lives in America without guns, or Kurds, or . . .

A fire sparked in Ali's eyes.

I am not foolish enough to follow my dreaming brother, Maman's favorite, who lived in the cinema since he was six and took the movies in like milk and thinks our dead mother will be proud of him for making it to America. Even if she were alive, she would only be proud of you. Maman was never proud of me.

Ali, you must come. Otherwise, if you stay, if you go back, you are dead.

Ali stood and walked away. He leaned against the wide entry of the hangar. His figure was small against the jungle, and he kept still, tilted with one hand on his hip, for a long time. Saladin kept focused on Ali as if, at any moment his brother could, on the strength of his will alone, evaporate from the hangar, from this island, from Saladin's life.

When Ali came back, the cold anger had gone from his body and his face. He walked casually and wore the soft smile he used to dole out gifts for their sisters. He shook his head back and forth, disbelieving.

Saladin jaan. Who would have guessed? The two of us? In Los Angeles? If that is the way it must be, that is the way. Every day I say let's stay, let's go back, but every day you say no, let's go, and we go. The gods must be on your side . . . who am I to resist?

If Saladin had known his whole life at that moment, had known every direction of all the dead before him and the details of the various futures ahead, he would have looked more carefully at his brother, questioned the sudden smile on his face and the flat, far-off eyes. But Saladin and everyone else asleep in the hangar knew only what they knew: that today they were here, locked in this purgatory, and tomorrow they would be up and gone to the next test, and Saladin felt a strong gladness fill his head and breast at the thought of his brother, his companion, his blood for all time, beside him now and tomorrow and the next day as they flew and then walked and then slept in their new American lives. Saladin wanted badly to embrace Ali. To hold his hand and feel his brother's flesh as some sort of promise.

Ali spread out on his cot and spoke to the ceiling.

Let us take what is given . . . The gods, just like Maman, were always on your side.

Ali closed his eyes.

Maybe you should sleep in the plane tonight. To make sure we have a place there tomorrow. We are surrounded by desperate men.

Saladin could not believe his brother's foresight, the light, ready thinking he had that had dragged since that first dash out of the wet valley, when all of Ali's steps had been heavy and every push forward was Saladin's heave.

Then we will know for sure that we are going. You will have secured a space.

Come with me, Ali! We can sleep together, they will know there are two of us . . .

Saladin's voice sounded like a child's and he stopped himself.

Ali smiled up at him.

Na, baba, I like it here. It is cool. I like the air of this place. Let me enjoy it for one last night. You go. Sleep. Dream of motorcycles and I will dream of . . . I don't know what I will dream of . . . girls. Brigitte Bardot.

But she is not Amreekayee, she is . . .

Ali turned over to face the far wall and yawned.

Yes, Saladin, I know. Please . . . let me make my own dreams.

A long platform slanted out and down from the back of the plane. Saladin walked quietly up and found a place between the boxes where he could stretch out his legs and lay down his shoulders.

For a long time his heart did not slow. Afraid the dull, hollow thuds of his heartbeat could be heard against the metal hull of the plane, he changed from one position to another and breathed in long, slow intervals. Saladin dropped his head and let in the heavy, marvelous thoughts of what it meant to have a brother: one who could walk ahead or behind and also right beside; another kind of self; another who is still you, with you, regardless of his life, obsessions, fates. Saladin let sleep drop him beneath the plane, below the soil of the island, deep into a center of the earth, where there is no spin.

LOVE AND ALL THE OPPOSITES

ENOUGH DAYS HAVE passed that few moments are first moments. In the month since he stumbled down the plank of the cargo plane, stomach full of island fish stew, Saladin has become, to his mind, American and moves about Los Angeles as if nothing in this new life could shock or surprise him. As if.

He is busy as he thought Americans would be busy, without pause or distraction, occupied by the many demands of his day. He wakes early to help Calderon with the first meal and even helps to clean before he catches the bus that takes him to the rug shop, where the rug seller meets him at the door with a cup of tea.

Thank you, Agha, but I just . . .

The rug seller hears none of it.

First we take tea. We must take tea. We have been starting with tea for thousands of years. Here. Take the tea, otherwise we turn into them.

He gestures out the windows with the enameled demitasse and grumbles.

Machines.

The days are made of dust and rugs—rolled, stacked, vacuumed, beaten—and by late afternoon Saladin is on his way to the cinema with cash in his pocket. It is always the same multiplex between Highland and La Brea, where if he does it right, he can watch two or even three films for the price of one. When he is finished, it is night, and the walk home is cool and Saladin is careful to stay away from bars and girls and the television sets that play face-out from glass storefronts. He keeps his head low so to make it home, to the bunk in Calderon's house, where he can sleep easy and orient his soul in the direction of another day, exactly the same, without memory or fear.

Like this, he triangulates between Wilshire, Highland, Vine and Ponderosa, and every step has its own destination, a face, a job, the evening's pleasure, and there is little risk of getting or being lost. No longer does he need to stop at the corner of Westwood and Santa Monica to stare in fascination at the billboard of the near-naked girl who smiles over her shoulder as a boy unties the knot that holds up a bikini that is forever *almost* slipping off. No longer does he have to look up and shout, Hello! My name is Saladin. Of the Ayyubids. Great hero of the Kurds. Conqueror of Richard the Lionheart himself. You are very pretty! All I need is the air that I breathe and to love you! Now the days are plain and she is plain in them, and Saladin walks underneath her enormousness, her *almost* nudity, and the warm glow of her eyes that seems directed at him and keeps on, past the tease of her shoulder, her eyes, the tease of her offerings, the tease of the tease of chance.

Soon the days make more than a month and near two months, and nothing has changed, not even the weather. There has not been one day of cloud, wind or rain, and Saladin wonders about the monotony of American weather. He asks the rug seller about snow and winter and spring rain, and the merchant stares at him with true curiosity.

But this is paradise, Saladin jaan. There is no snow in paradise . . .

At breakfast Saladin asks Calderon, and the landlord laughs at him and all his teeth show.

What's the matter, my friend? You don't like sunny California?

Two months pass, and Saladin is certain he does not like it. The constant sun is an agitation; its brightness shines down on the city of metal, chrome, aluminum and glass, which then shine back up so the world is bright from below as well as above and vibrates like some loud off-key hum. Worse are the shadows that plaster themselves to Saladin at every moment of every day, everywhere he goes. He wishes for a cloudy day to relieve him of this constant dark stamp or some great shade that will erase the print of himself that follows and leads, follows and leads, and does not, except in the cinema, leave him alone. Even the night has no reprieve with its fluorescent lights and streetlamps, and Saladin can always find the version of this silhouette that sticks to him like a dim, dull friend. Less than three months since he has arrived and he spends every hot, white day planning for the dark, cool cinema, where he is alone at last, a man separate and alone.

The relief is short. After the cinema he must adjust his eyes to the bright night streets, where the light pours off the marquees, down from the neon of stores and bars, blasts from cars's headlights and washes all over Hollywood Boulevard, where men and women and children gather to perform their contests of stillness, feats of gymnastics, dances and tricks, while beneath them dark second selves shift about the pavement like a flattened circus. There are tourists, Americans from another part of America Saladin has yet to imagine, who walk hand in hand with their families, their shadows forming the patterns of cutout dolls. Even the women who gather just in front of the cinema in restless postures of anxiety and serenity, boredom and agitation, anchor their shadows down with the sharp spikes of their high high heels.

Saladin has seen these women early in the evening when the sun is low and their shadows are long, he has heard their talk about the money tonight and the money last week and the police two weeks ago and *No, no, not again. He wears a brown jacket. Know him by the brown jacket, honey. Watch out for that man.* After enough nights he has seen their details, the spaces between their heel and shoe, their breast and bra, he has seen them hide in the alley between the cinema and the house of wax, where their shadows are thrown on the bricks behind them, overlarge, tawdry and mocking. Sometimes they are scattered out at the far corners of the block where they pace near and into traffic, bend over and lean through passenger windows to see and be seen, negotiate and lure, and their shadows lie out to one side just beneath the tires of the stopped car.

In the first month they approached him with regularity.

Hey, honey! Hooooney, why don't you stop here a minute.

No one leaves Hollywood without a suck from a star.

Special rate for you, honey, we love Mexicans.

What's your name? . . . What? . . . What kind of name is that? We gonna call you Sal.

Heeeey, Saaaal. My name is Maria, or Marilyn if you like, or Betty. I am Zsa Zsa . . .

Giant and stilted and teetering, they circled around him with their swarm of offers. He tried not to catch their eyes, not to stare too long at their presentations of fantasy and desire: the glossed lips, exposed backs and hips with tattoos of hearts and roses and children's faces as authentic as old photographs. They walked about laughing and sad, and Saladin pushes past, unable to find in them, on them, near them, some safe corner to tuck his desire.

No, thank you. Please. No, thank you.

Behind him they always shouted, *Saaaal, Saaal. Come on, Saaaaaal needs a suck*, and other things that had the timbre of calls between children at play, at once happy and mean.

There is a night when the film is terrible. A wealthy girl and a wealthy boy. A love story. Death. The boy is weak in his grief, and Saladin does not respect him. He leaves the cinema annoyed for reasons he does not bother to tease apart. As on every night, the women are at the end of the block, and as on every night they throw him a few calls, and once he crosses the street they leave him alone.

On this night a new girl stands far out from the rest, by herself in front of the windows of a closed flower shop, and far from the traffic of cars and men on the street. There is an urge, quick and biting and rare, to see her face. Saladin tries to pass her to leave the urge behind and take his foul mood to his bunk so that he can sleep and wake up again and start anew. He disciplines himself again and again not to stop, not to look, but he cannot resist and casts half a look at her, and it is done, she is known. He stares without tact or guile and she stares back.

Yes?

She smokes a cigarette and speaks the one word. Saladin does not know how to look at her and puts his hands in his back pockets in the posture of a confident American man, and only then does he dare take her in, the chin and cheeks and lips and sky-blue eyes, everything held up and high. It is the face of women he has known: the mother, the sister, the beloved, but lighter, without color or consequence or weight. To speak with her he must tell himself she is from before, from the land and life he had before this one, where he had a brother, father and friends. His courage wanes and he speaks to her as if she were the billboard.

Hello. My name is Saladin . . .

She smokes quietly and looks at the full form of him and laughs until he stops speaking and nearly begins to cry. She answers in Farsi.

Salaam Saladin. Halleh shomah chetoreh?

He can and cannot believe it and tries to collect all his scattered thoughts, to put them away and impress her, but he is clumsy and overexcited and talks in a hasty, childish stream.

Where are you from? When did you come here? Where do you live? Why are you . . .

— — —

Her eyes are alive and her mouth is wide across her teeth, and Saladin steps back to see her small shoulders, the tight bra, the soft stomach and the thin legs that stretch all the way down to the shadow just beneath her feet.

This is your work? You do this?

Her smile collapses and she drops the cigarette down and steps on it. She moves toward him and shakes her light hair out of her face.

If you would like, I will go to the cinema with you.

Saladin looks around at the street as if the lights, the tourists and the other prostitutes could explain this woman to him.

She clears her throat and asks again.

Take me to the cinema. Please. It has been a long time since I saw a film. You can tell me what they are saying. Please. It is right there.

Almost three months, and the routine has changed. Saladin watches the first movie alone and, at the cost of paying for the second film, leaves the cinema to meet her in front of the flower shop, and together they see one or two more, depending on the mood. Afterward he buys her ice cream and she eats it with manners, but Saladin cannot help watching as she attaches her lips to the cream. She talks often and easily and with a girlish joy that maybe, he thinks, she has held back just for him.

The ice cream is just like in Kabul. The same sweet taste.

Yes. But better.

Yes, the ice cream may be better—she laughs—but the movies are the same.

Like this: the cinema, the ice cream, the walk up and down Highland and the handshakes good-night. They learn each other in increments. They walk up and down the boulevard like tourists, watch the entertainments on display and are two of the millions, a young man and a young woman together, in the city at night, and for this Saladin sleeps deep and solid through every night.

One evening they pass two young men at the start of a fistfight, and Saladin pulls Nafaz by the elbow but she resists and stands closer to watch.

All fighting is the same. See. Look. One will punch and the other will take the punch, and then they will reverse it, and he will try and the other will move away. In my mother's village there was a time when Russians and the mujahideen punched each other with all their strength at the same time. That village no longer exists. You can only find it now on the oldest maps.

At the sight of a mother and daughter walking hand in hand, Nafaz talks of her mother and the rosewater perfumes she used after her baths.

Only the loveliest fragrances. She was a very beautiful woman.

And just as instantly a small boy is her little brother, and she talks without stop about his night frights and hate of lentils and their shared afternoon naps where she would start a story for him to finish.

But he never did. He always fell asleep during my half. Silly.

Saladin waited for her to continue, to tell him more, to take him back to a place like the place he had come from. Sometimes she did and sometimes she didn't, and he told himself not to ask for more.

* * *

One night they see the movie of a starving shark. Another night they see a movie of space travel and planets with two moons. They see a sad film where the beautiful woman leaves her husband to be with her lover and loses her family and home, and in the dark Nafaz takes Saladin by the hand and he holds her small palm, as warm and soft as he imagined it, and tries to keep his breath steady and strong.

When the film is finished, she does not let go and leads him away from the cinema and the crowds up a side street and then up a small, winding road where the houses are barely lit, and soon they are climbing and breathless and silent. At the end of the road there is a park, and before it the city spreads out, lights from the mountains to the dark sea. Saladin stares over it, tries to know his here and there, his work and bed, but there are only lights, spilled and scattered across the huge basin, and he can only find in it beauty and more beauty. He holds tightly to Nafaz's hand and she holds tightly back.

I have been with seven men. Two Mexicans, a black. The rest were Americans, I guess.

The city glimmers and he cannot turn away from it to see her face as she says what she says.

And still my life here is safer than my life in Kabul. I have made many sacrifices to be here . . . this is the way.

She talks, with wandering eyes and nervous hands, as if she were telling the city, but only Saladin listens. The story is long and slow and she starts at the beginning, at the place from which nothing could stay the same, on the afternoon she heard that her mother and father and two brothers had been killed under a Russian bomb.

I was away, at my uncle's house in Kabul, taking school exams for the fifth form. He came to me outside the library and said, It is gone. Your family. Your town. You live here now, with me. My entire family, in one moment . . .

She spoke without sadness and explained situations as if they had no emotion.

In the beginning he was kind. He sold my father's goods in the market, and after a while there was nothing to sell and my uncle grew poor and angry and after a few weeks cursed me and said I had brought him bad luck. The mujahideen would come to our door and promise money, guns, food, if my uncle fought with them. They said he was a good Muslim, but to be a great Muslim he should join with them. They said I was a tempting girl and that he should make sure I covered and did not dishonor him. They offered him great sums of money every time they visited our house. We had less and less, food, electricity, tea, and finally when we had nothing, he took what they gave him and burned my clothes and told me to wear a sheet over my head and body at all times. I did as he said, and for some reason that only made him angrier.

From the broad valley the sirens of two fire trucks sing around them for a time and she stops talking. Saladin feels her hand grow moist in his. He tries to pull it out but her grip is tight.

I think it was pleasurable for him to beat me. He had no other power, and at first all he did was force me to cook for him, to clean and lie in his bed. He told me the cinema was forbidden but I disobeyed. I would make him a heavy, heavy lunch, full of stews and naan, and when the house filled with his snores, I snuck out to the afternoon movies at one of the last cinemas in Kabul. I watched the women, I sat and waited through film after film just to watch the women. What beauties.

She looks ahead of her, her eyes light with some old joy, the same face Saladin has seen her wear in the cinema, concentrated with delight.

Bergman. Doris Day. Lizbet Taylor, Grace Kelly. Gina Lollobrigida. Even the Hindi women. They were like royalty to me, and even though I was just a girl, I knew that royalty was inside me too, because one day I would be a woman, beautiful like them. I had seen myself in the mirror, I had seen myself in the eyes of men who stared at me. I knew I had a wealth of some sort.

When she speaks, Saladin first hears the pretty lilt of her voice, then the odd Afghani Farsi, and then, only a few seconds later, is he able to hear her meaning. She talks about her uncle, his rabid devotion, the letter he received from the American consulate that thanked him for his cooperation with the Taliban, offered him a green card and a free move to the United States.

But the monster did not know how to read. I took the letter and kept it, and soon after that he became very sick. Amazingly sick. No one knew where the illness came from. He would not eat, could not sleep. He sweated through each night in high fevers and the doctors were confused: *Such a young man, so much vigor* . . . He would get better, gain weight and walk the garden, and the doctors seemed sure that with rest and the care of a beautiful, dutiful niece, full recovery was inevitable. But I did not take care of him. If he called for water, I pretended that I did not hear. If he cried out after a fall, I watched him struggle to stand and remembered the nights he took his heavy hand to my face, my chest and shoulders and the mornings he pressed himself into me and cursed my mother all the while. I made his meals, his tea, his bed. Who is to say I did not put in too much medicine or not enough? People, the neighbors, the men who would come to visit him, just shook their heads and said things like *Look what war will do . . . bechareh . . .* Then one day, like the sick do, he died. There were few mourners. If anyone suspected anything, they did not say.

Her hand is like a vise, as if the skin and muscle have been pressed away. She holds Saladin tightly now, bone to bone.

The American consulate passed his green card to me. They knew I was an orphan, a woman without husband or family stuck in a destroyed city with no hope. I left that same week. There was little packing to do, no one to tell good-bye.

She lights a cigarette, and the fire travels back and forth to her face, and Saladin can see how light it really is, in feature and color and weight, and on this night it seems nearly buoyant, as if it were filled with the smoke of the cigarette and nothing else. Behind them the noise of small footsteps catches their attention, and they turn to see an old Mexican woman with a bucket of roses. She does not smile, does not increase her speed or pull up the shawl that drags behind her on the ground.

Para la señora. La enamorada.

The roses in the bucket are dried at the edges and wilted through the stems. All these weeks Saladin has bought Nafaz cinema tickets, ice cream, and waited for the moment to touch her, to pull her face to his and feel the press of lips, but the moment never came. He walked toward it every day and wondered at his patience, at the small resistance he had to taking what he thought was slowly being offered and now under the stare of the Mexican woman, it becomes clear. Saladin tries to pull his hand from hers, but Nafaz does not let go. Through the hand he feels her hope—for the bouquet, the gift of flowers, for his forgiveness—as it exits her body and enters his. He shakes his head no and the old Mexican walks away with same small steps and long, dragged shawl.

Saladin pulls Nafaz by the hand and moves them down the hill, down through the neighborhood and back onto the streets of Hollywood, where the lights are bright and the noise of cars and people weaves between them. He shakes off her hand and steps back to look at her, to assess and understand and regard her as they are to each other: familiars; a family of halves; brother and sister. He sees the lightness leave her face and follows it as it drains all the way down her slim body to the tiny heels that stab the long, thin shadow that sways behind her, darker than dark. Nafaz returns his glare, and though Saladin cannot see the man she sees, he knows the life he has lived, the person he is, the ways he too has cheated the old homes and the old loves for this American night. She takes a step back and then another and then turns and, without a word, is gone. Saladin walks against her, away, and they disappear, this man and this woman, into a happy Hollywood and all the night's noise.

If he told her, what would he say?

I loved the cinema too? I was a child of the cinema just like you . . . I have done terrible things, left behind my life, to live in the cinema.

How would he say it?

Where does he start? Istanbul? In the dusty town? In the green valley, in his mother's lap, in his boyhood bed? As far back the womb or the womb before that?

Would he tell a clear story with a beginning, middle and end or sum it up in a sentence, thrown off and haphazard?

Does anger shake his voice or will he cry?

Does he confess that he left behind a brother for this Los Angeles? Would he say his brother left him?

Hollywood is far behind now, and Saladin walks briskly through an unfamiliar neighborhood of enormous houses and steep, long hills. There are no people, only lawns like rugs and ornate streetlamps. The more he thinks to say it, the how and when and which way to tell her, the faster his feet move, just as on that first night when he ran to outpace his nerves, to keep off the shock of survival. How did it happen? Perhaps it didn't happen at all? Maybe he dreamed it? Maybe he was asleep in the hull of the plane, dreaming. Yes. That much is true: he was dreaming. When he tells it to her, that is where he will start.

I dream.

I have always been dreaming.

That night I slept in the hull of the plane, I dreamt.

The metal of the plane was cold and refused to warm from his body heat. In his half sleep he dreamed of a Los Angeles he had not yet seen, every street corner and shop window and taxicab filled with faces from the mountain town. In the episodes of shivering wakefulness he could hear Ali, just a few meters away, awake, quietly singing the Beatles song. And so it was as it had been all the days of this journey, one brother waiting for the night to push him forward, and the other waiting for the same night to take them back.

When the first noise of jeeps and trucks came, Saladin tried to incorporate their throttle and the loud shouts into his frigid dreams, but they would not fit. He woke and crawled slowly to the opening in the back of the plane and saw the ten, maybe twelve men who roved about the hangar in uniforms with white sashes, each with a small, portable light in one hand and tiny pistol in the other. They kicked the men awake and off the floor, and when they had pushed everyone up against the far wall, the demands began. They spoke in a language that was neither English nor the language of the island, but both mixed to senselessness. The white sashes pushed at the men with their loud voices and flat hands.

Name! *Nomeh*?

From? From? Afghan? Iran? Turkey?

The recently arrived men were still sleepy and had not yet woken into indignation, into the refusal or the sharp wit that would help them to lie, to save themselves. They answered without guile.

Reza Amanizabeh.

From!?

Iran.

Esfandear Tafreshi.

From!

Iran.

Alone?

Yes.

Name!

Houseein Oshalinpour.

Alone?

No. With cousin.

. . . Father.

. . . Uncle, here.

And on and on down the line. Saladin crouched farther back into the plane, so to wait out this terror, to hide until the mass was gone and dawn came and the plane would take him up into some questionless space. He heard the voice of the light-eyed father, and then, the hushed sobs of his light-eyed son and saw a white sash turn the hand light on them both.

Where!

— — —

Where?!

The pistol waved just beneath the man's chin, and in the bright light the color of his eyes opened and shone as if, with enough illumination, you could see into and through them.

The light-eyed man looked into the tiny bulb and answered.

Iran.

Bem.

. . . where we will be killed.

The white sash pushed them aside, and Saladin saw a group was forming, and all the men, except for him and his brother, were in it.

When he tells her, he will tell her honestly. He will say, My brother saved me from the raid that he arranged. My brother, my only brother, Ali, was willing, maybe wanting, to see me go. He could do without me. Saladin will say it as he feels it. I had a brother who abandoned me. I had a brother, he was kind and cruel.

In the hangar a single voice shouted.

Ali Khourdi! Ali Khourdi!

They knew his name. They shouted it the same way his boyhood friends shouted it on the soccer field in the mountain town—urgently, with confidence, excited for the signature long, clean pass—and for a moment Saladin closed his eyes against this dark chaos and waited for the image of that game, the green grass, the gray, open skies of his hometown. In that world he heard Ali's voice.

Yes. I am here.

Everyone here? Is this all the men?

Yes.

You are sure? All men here?

Yes.

And you? No brother?

No.

The boy today? The boy, in the town? Who?

No one.

Alone?

Yes. No brother.

Some of the gathered men made noises as if to say yes, yes, he does, he has a brother. The light-eyed man said nothing, and Saladin saw him cover his son's mouth, but the others let it be known there was one more, there was another. The hand lights shot through the hangar like a dozen roving stars and floated over bunched blankets, sacks and pushed-off shoes, tossed aside blankets, maps and prayer beads.

Where!

The man demanded, and all the lights returned to Ali's face. In the brightness Saladin saw his brother, as he had known him his whole life, as he was in the square the morning the Kurdish men were sentenced to death, the same calm eyes beneath heavy brows, the flat line of a set, satisfied mouth.

I have no brother.

The white sash waited, and the sequestered men waited, and Saladin waited, and then, just like that, all that had been spoken was true.

Bem. To the buses.

They pushed the men onto the buses, and the hangar emptied of all sound and light and breath. Saladin kept his eyes on Ali, who did not get on the bus with the rest of them but took a seat in the backseat of the jeep, where he accepted a cigarette from a white sash. Saladin stared at his brother but could not bring himself to leave the plane, to jump out and yell, But you said you would come! Why are you not coming! Together. We have to go together. You will die in Iran!

But his body did not move. To call him would mean going back, being known, arrested, redirected from Los Angeles to some other place. Saladin let every part of him stick to the surface of the metal hull, and where he should have felt sadness or confusion or fear, Saladin felt only a long, fierce cold. He curled into himself for heat, and still his body shivered and his teeth clicked and he shook and sweated and pulled his shoulders tight against his ears. He had no clothes but the shirt and pants and shoes he had put on in the dark the morning their father yelled them awake days? weeks? months?

ago. He had no money or suitcase or passport, no promise of a bed tomorrow or the day after that. And if he died on this night, a chunk of frozen flesh, he had chosen not to have a brother who could say, His name is. His age was. He was born in this town. Our mother was. Our father was. Yes. He was my brother.

That night there was no sleep. Saladin shivered and tried to find warmth in his armpits, in his crotch, in the breath he pushed into cupped hands. When the plane took off just after dawn, he barely noticed that he had just done as the birds did and taken to the sky. He held to himself and kept quiet, the only smuggled man aboard, a stowaway who would never do the two months of factory work, but who would, instead, do the work of untangling a great deceit between brothers, for the rest of his life.

For a week Saladin avoids the intersection of Hollywood and Vine. He stays late at the warehouse and begs the rug seller to give him more work, more hours, so he can make more money. The rug seller asks no questions and obliges, and by the end of the week nearly no rugs are left to vacuum or stack or roll or ship, and Saladin asks Calderon if there are things he can do around the house.

Calderon shakes his head.

No, no, *hermano*. Relax. You work too much. This is California! All America comes here to go on vacation. Take a break.

When Saladin wakes up the next morning, a ten-dollar bill is underneath his door. It is casually crumpled as if dropped. Saladin knows better but puts the bill in his pocket anyway and skips breakfast, embarrassed to look Calderon in the eye. With his pockets full of money he walks through the city, goes in and out of his day at the shop and then back to the corner with the multiplex and the tourists and the girls who call out.

Hey, Sal . . . hey, Sal. How come you aren't going to see your movie? You ready for another kind of show? It's about time . . .

He misses the five o'clock show he would see alone and then the seven he would watch with her and stands in front of the closed flower shop and waits. Just after dark a bus groans to a stop at the end of the block, and she walks to him slowly without a smile. Her face is impatient. A shield of anger braces her across the shoulders, chest and hips.

Yes?

I have brought . . .

He begins in Farsi, then switches to English.

For you.

He tries to hand the stack of bills, almost ironed, more American money than he has ever had, to her. In his mind she takes it and they walk to get ice cream and he explains to her all that he has thought about, all that he is ready to tell. He tells her the events of the night he left his brother to the police so he could come to America. She forgives him. He tells her he does not know where Ali is today, if he is alive or dead or where, and it is bad for a brother not to know. Isn't it bad that a brother does not know? She forgives him. He explains he cannot love her the way the men and women in the cinema love, that they are too alike, brother and sister, and he wants an American woman, someone who has not forgone all family and love. Someone new. It is what his mother would want, now that he has made it all this way. Nafaz smiles and accepts his explanation and forgives him. In his mind he buys her another ice cream.

But there is only the life outside his mind. The cars and streetlamps and a woman who does not reach out to take the bills. Saladin thinks to explain.

I was dreaming. That night, when they raided the hangar, I was asleep. Dreaming . . .

The impatience on her face turns to disbelief and then disgust. The money stays out in front of them, between them, and she does not take her hands out of the pockets of her jacket to accept it.

I am not a whore for you. You cannot pay me.

Saladin extends his arm completely. He does not know how much life costs in America. He knows the price of the cinema, the price of food, the rent on his bunk and breakfast at Calderon's house, and he offers her all the cash anyway, thinks it is enough to keep her from this corner and the dead ends of a life that should have a few beginnings. He cannot love her and so he thrusts the money toward her, and she steps back and then back again and then turns away and walks down the street.

No . . . no . . . it is so you can stop. The work. Here, it will help. For you. I cannot be with you because you are . . . and I am . . . and it is not new . . . But here. This money is for you. Here. A gift for you! Please! Nafaz!

She walks away with a quick step, as if her name were not Nafaz, as if she were another woman with another past and another future in which she is very very busy, with a million places to go.

It is near four months and there is a new routine. After work Saladin takes a long route from the rug warehouse to Calderon's neighborhood and does not pass the tourists or the multiplex or the stars and handprints and footprints in the sidewalk at Hollywood and Vine. In the evenings he eats a quiet dinner with the other men and refuses their offers of soccer games or pulls from their tequila and goes to the cinema down the street. All the movies are in Spanish, and he watches one after the next and takes in the great fights and greater romances and happy endings of pure rapture.

ECUMENOPOLIS

IN TRUTH, WE were not alone. No matter how much we thought or felt or wanted it to be otherwise, it was not, and everywhere we looked there were others. They did not share our language or our looks, but in many ways they are more similar to us than our own families.

We saw them in our children's classrooms, heard their English just as shaky as our own, with attitudes just as defensive and defeated, and faces washed over by the same disbelief that here, in these small and colorful rooms, our children came each day to sing and learn and believe things we ourselves did not yet know.

We saw them at the immigration offices, in large waiting rooms where all of our hearts beat over important documents and we reminded ourselves there was no going back, and if it came to it, pleading, in this case, was not shameful. In that long boredom where we waited for new numbers and new identities, we might have talked, exchanged stories, a family name, a country of origin, all of it hesitant and minimal because really, once we knew we were not alone, we did not have to tell each other about the why or when or how come.

Nevertheless, as it is with people everywhere, stories were told. We told ours to them and listened to the accounts of the Vietnamese, who traveled by boatload, men and women and children, sun-blistered and dehydrated, spotted by helicopter and saved by navy warship. We listened to the story of the Honduran gardener who took his trip on the top of train cars that traveled north through Mexico to the border in Laredo. *If there was violence, a thief, a person went crazy with a knife, a fight, there was nowhere to go. We could not jump off.* The Soviet Armenians told us that the central government discriminated against them, erratically stopped shipments of medicine, baby formula, teachers. *They did not care if we died. So we left.* We listened because it made us feel better, and sometimes worse, but regardless it made us feel as if we were among company of some kind. We told our own stories and we were heard.

Imagine our shock when we heard or read that in 1982 alone nine thousand documented foreign immigrants moved to Los Angeles. Here we had come all this way to make ourselves in the mold of Steve McQueen and Farrah Fawcett, and instead we found a city full of our similar selves, not in language and looks, but in fate and circumstance. Imagine our shock when, after some years, we noticed that we had not at all become Americans in that vein, that there was no chance of such shape-shifting, but instead America, California, Los Angeles, became a bit more like us. Entire stretches and blocks of storefront windows were etched in Mandarin, Korean,

Farsi, Thai, and the smells that came out of the kitchens belonged to ancient kitchens, and the spices and roots were grown in bathtubs, gallon jugs, coffee cans. The city molded to our superstitions, our sacred behaviors, and when a bus hit an El Salvadorian boy on the corner of Mariposa, the sidewalk took all the flowers and candles and statues of the Virgin Mary the hands of the devout laid down. There were parks where we felt good, at ease, where we could take our walks, hold our auspicious-day festivities, enjoy a cigarette alone on a bench under the dappled light of a plane tree and mistake the moment for another just like it in Tehran/Bombay/Seoul/Juárez/Hanoi.

And each day came with a greater possibility of looking out at a world, once foreign to us, and hoping that, with luck, the group of us—aliens, immigrants, temporary residents—could fashion a new nation in our own image, and we made sure to match eyes with the others, unlike us in language or looks, and recognize that though it might have felt otherwise, we were not alone. On sunny days, sometimes that was enough.

As the world outside of our home grew warm and familiar, the lives lived inside those homes took on a strange and hostile hum. Our children began to misbehave. Notes were sent home from school, from the play yard that emphasized their *tantrums, quick temper, overreaction to simple childish taunts*. At home things were no better. They looked into our faces and mocked our accents, which were still, at that point, their accents as well. They could not stand our questions as easy as Hello, how are you today? What is that drawing you have there? And they pushed away our offers of help, our food and jokes, the names we gave them and our habitual, ceaseless affection. You kiss too much, they said as they wiped their cheeks with the palms of their hands. Americans don't kiss like this. It's gross. What was gross? What was that word? Who were these children? We ask ourselves. They were not the same children we had in Iran. You liked my kisses before when we were in Iran? They push us away and then shamelessly beg for skateboards and video games and makeup and freedom, and when we shake our heads, they drop into a sullen behavior for which we have no recourse but anger, and we are quick with it, honest and clean.

Joonam, we say sweetly, remember I control your fate. We could have easily left you behind. Remember, your visa alone cost us a hand and foot. It is true that they would not make fun of your name, yes. They would use it instead to call you out to the army, where you might have ended up like Arash's cousin, no arms, no legs, dead and nameless on the Iraqi desert floor.

And if it's not the children that seem strange, then it is the old people. They complain about the traffic (which is no different from Tehran), the water (also no different), the smog (again, the same). Sometimes they even complain about the salt. Where is the flavor? they bemoan. What a bechareh am I? To live a whole life of delight so that I can die a nobody in the land of plastic. They enjoy exaggeration. We suffer their drama. Out of respect we cannot admonish them, we must sit and listen and wonder, Who are you? Who, Maman jaan, are you? And, Baba joon, where has the man I loved gone?

Then there are quiet questions asked from one soul to another like the questions we ask our beloved when we cannot sleep and our beloved lies beside us, our closest intimate, now a stranger to us in the night. How can I know you in this new life and how can you know me? We are no longer the man and the woman in the wedding photo. That world no longer exists. We are not the couple in the cinema or at the hospital after the birth of our first child. How far have we traveled that you, my heart, are so unfamiliar to me?

Night noises leak in through the windows and fill the dark. We concentrate on them with the hope that somewhere through the shouts and car horns, sirens and laughs, we can find sleep, but all that comes are the questions that chase our million tails like a frenzied beast. Who are you, love of mine, similar to me in language and looks? How will I come to love you in this new life? How will you know to love me?

DEVILS, PICNICS, POETS

SOME DAYS THE rug seller wakes up in Los Angeles, and some days he wakes up in a city where he no longer lives. On this day Saladin finds him outside the plate-glass window with his name on it, the store behind him dark and closed. His eyes are frantic with delight, and his mouth buzzes with some constant mutterings.

It is the thirteenth day, the devil's day, the day the devil comes to work, to the house, comes and takes the luck for the year away.

He paces before the storefront, and when Saladin arrives, he clasps his shoulders with both hands.

Finally, my boy! We must go! It is the thirteenth day, don't you know! We must go before the devil finds us and curses our fortune. Come come. Yallah!

Outside the store the rug seller seems shorter. He walks ahead of Saladin with the punchy gestures of a horse-mounted warrior leading a thousand horse-mounted warriors. In reality only Saladin follows, and as the two men stand and wait for the crosswalk signal, only one has his feet firmly on the cement corner of Flower and Central Avenue, while the other stands on some cherished corner in Tehran, impatient, en route to his favorite park.

At the park it is just as Saladin has tried to forget it was: blankets enormous enough to fit a dozen relatives, steel and copper pots of stew, sabzi from the sofre, countless cards, kites, charcoal and cigarettes. Somewhere far away, the thump of a daf, and nearby the intricate sounds of a doumbac. In the well of what was, the water rises to the top, rises to what is, and the old place pours over to cover the new place, and though Saladin has done his best to avoid this kind of drowning, today he fails. The park here today is fragrant like there, and it is bright here today as it was, on spring days, there. Here too the men and women are gathered just out of the devil's reach on this thirteenth day of the new year, the first unlucky day when all must be emptied, homes, offices and stores, so when the devil comes to find and taint you, no one is around. Saladin walks sourly among the happy families like a man pushed back, a man not allowed to move one millimeter east or one millimeter west and forced to keep stiff above an earth that spins beneath such that all these weeks and months of movement have taken him nowhere at all.

The rug seller is here beside him and then away, on a blanket tasting the saffron pudding offered by a jolly mother, and then he is beside Saladin again, with introductions and boasts.

Yes, he works for me. Khourdi. A good man, strong with the heavy rugs, but thinks he's too handsome for the work, wants to be a famous actor.

The women smile and the men laugh, and Saladin does not

shake one hand, does not meet one eye, embarrassed by their familiar faces, their familiar smells, dismayed by the familiar beauty of their daughters as they are offered up to him: flowers plucked too early from far soils, some faces flush with the last of beauty, some already wilting under the hot California sun. It is just a little more than a year after the revolution, and the arrived are gathered to remember and forget. Saladin does not want to recognize them as his own and does not want to be recognized as one of them. He tells himself he sees nothing of his mother's beauty in the faces of the mothers, hears nothing of his father's hearty laugh in the men gathered, shoeless and cross-legged, on the blankets all around. Regardless, the smell of kebab is the same, the friendly calls of *Mobarak* and *Befaymin* are exact, and each smile is open and familiar, as if Los Angeles were Tehran and all are doing as they have always done. He leaves the picnics without eating and stifles the hunger that rises through his belly and throat.

At the far end of the park a set of swings rock back and forth and let loose dark, aggravating squeaks. Saladin walks to them. Two girls fly and sink, fly and sink, while between them an old man stands, the wisps of his white hair blown by the wind of pumping legs, soaring shoulders and billowing skirts. He is without wrinkles and has skin the color of sand in the shade; he stands still and moves only his mouth, and around him men and women listen to the words as they come out, hold their elbows, their cigarettes, their sorrow and longing. To the rhythm of the unoiled swings he recites:

You think your monarch's palace of more worth
Than him who fashioned it and all the earth.
The home we seek is in eternity;
The truth we seek is like a shoreless sea,
Of which your paradise is but a drop.
The ocean can be yours; why should you stop
Beguiled by dreams of evanescent dew?
The secrets of the sun are yours, but you
Content yourself with motes trapped in its beams
Turn to what truly lives, reject what seems—
Which matters more, the body or the soul?
Be whole: desire and journey to the whole.

Saladin looks at the girls, who swing back and forth beside the poet in high, even arcs, eyes tearing from the wind. Lucky the child who knows so little about here and less about there. Lucky the child left to fling her legs, let air and aspiration fill her heart. Unlucky the gathered crowd; men with heads bowed and women with hearts clenched, grandmothers who smack lips in disbelief over every bite: Doesn't taste the same, will never taste the same, how can it ever taste the same?

Damned be the poet who counsels them in the infinite, the whole, the ecstatic, who tries to move the souls stuck in these bodies that force them to blankets, food, each other, the recreation and re-creation of home on this thirteenth day of spring when they must jump, leap, out from under the devil's grasp, out from the old homes, loved homes where left-behind mother and sisters must shroud themselves in the streets and sons and fathers line up to die in the war. Saladin sees himself among them, on the bright green grass, under the warm sun, just out from under the devil's grasp, out and away from a country that blackens behind them, and knows they are, swinging girl and grandmother alike, deaf to the poet's call to go, go home.

Saladin looks about for the rug seller to excuse himself from the celebrations, but in the sea of men on blankets, he is hard to find. Saladin has almost given up when he sees Noori on a blanket surrounded by women. A blond-haired woman seems to be his wife, and the two girls are a few years younger than Saladin. They are telling what seems to be a long joke. He forces himself forward to give his thanks, make his excuse and say his good-bye, but it is not easy because the rug seller is happier than he has ever been and invites Saladin to taste his wife's famous sholeh zarde.

My boy! You must try it!

Noori offers up a spoonful of the sweet, yellow rice dessert, and Saladin remembers it was the same one his mother, and all the women of Iran, made on special occasions.

Such delicate texture. You must try it. She does not use too much cinnamon like the rest. And meet my daughters. Azar and Yasamine.

The two girls look up at Saladin as he chews and swallows. He tries not to look back, but the youngest one catches his glance with her tremendous lips and her father's joyful eyes. He tries for a smile, but nothing happens on his face, and embarrassed, he makes excuses and walks away, tossing behind him a series of quick, odd good-byes.

These Kurds, so moody and serious, always at war with something . . .

The voice of the rug seller's wife follows Saladin as he steps between blankets and hands and feet and the left-behind toys of children distracted by other things.

He moves past the tall glass buildings and does not stop. He roves the streets with eyes for some sensation of excitement, something anonymous and fast that will be American and nothing else, but it is midday midweek and only men and women in formal clothes are walking in and out, back and forth, as if on predestined rails. He finds a street that goes along a dry concrete river whose cracked, slanted edges sprout tall yellow grass. The concrete is covered in images and letters, the script bloated, and the illustrations show anatomies vulgar and unbelievable. Saladin finds a low bridge and follows it over the dry expanse. He stands at the center and looks down onto the concrete and wishes badly for the river to run so he can take the long, clean jump.

THE WAIT. THE WANT

NOT UNTIL A baby is born.

Not until your dead are buried beneath this ground.

Only then can you say that you belong to a place or claim that a place belongs to you.

We overhear this from some mouth or other, and just like that it is impossible to forget; no matter how hard we try to shake it out of our ears, like trapped water it just won't go.

So comically, desperately, with the bravado of heroes, some of us started fucking.

It if takes a baby to belong here, then a baby it will be!

An American baby, yes, but who cares?

We will teach him the old tongue, feed him the old food, and next month, next year, next lifetime, when all of this is over, we will simply take him back home.

He won't even remember his life here.

We announced such things and set about to seduce, to want, to join bodies in hope. We took off our early armor and allowed ourselves to be seduced and wanted and filled with hope.

Comically and then desperately and then against our better selves, a few of us even looked about at the elders and wondered, God forbidding of course, who would be the first to die? Like the poor coffin maker in a town without illness or death, our curious glances were tantamount to evil. They were already old, these grandmothers and grandfathers dragged halfway across the world because they couldn't be left behind, and we looked carefully at them to see if they had grown older. And they had. Since their arrival, the wrinkles had spread deeper and farther about their faces, they leaned in heavier on their crutches, they smoked more and spoke less.

Poor things, we said. And some of us thought about how nice it would be to wash the body, put it in the ground and stand over the fresh dirt, fresh American dirt, and say to ourselves, this square is ours. If nothing else, he is folded into the earth and so this small piece of earth belongs to us. We thought fondly of the ceremonies that followed the death. The third-day and the seventh-day and the fortieth-day gathers when families would come together around the grave and then take to the house of a relative to eat and drink and be among one another. We waited as the elders continued to shuffle among us, and we took the best care of them and tried not to let our thoughts wander back around the sayings, attributed to no one, that circled in our heads, a birth . . . a death . . . only then . . . belong . . . belong . . . belong.

Time passed, regardless. Babies came as they do, without any concern for parents or place, and we rejoiced, glad for their instant innocence, for our own new chances, for this life made of love and possibility that would fasten us to this country if only by merit of an American birth certificate that guaranteed life, liberty, the pursuit of happiness and other promises that were never made to us.

Not long after that the deaths came too. The oldest of us ended their days in rooms as foreign to them as the food and water that settled in their guts. We washed their bodies, oiled them with rose water and wrapped them in muslin that we bought from the Ethiopian fabric stores. We placed them in the heavy wooden box required by law, lacquered and glazed on the outside and plush on the inside, and lowered the boxes into the ground. It was not as we expected. The ceremonies came and went and we gathered at the green graves and the land did not feel like ours at all. We could not claim the grave, and it looked up at us dully, indistinguishable from all the graves around it, and we wondered why we thought a death would help. The old kept dying and we kept our eyes fastened to the ground, ashamed of our selfish curiosities and the silly superstitions in sayings.

Not until Neusha Farrahi.

Not until Neusha did we feel as if we belonged here. As if someone had finally died in a manner that tied us to this place. On this, regardless of our politics or money or loyalties, we agreed.

He was a bookseller. His father, his whole family, had long been persecuted under the Shah for their bohemian, leftist-leaning politics. Finally in 1980, with nearly a million other Iranians, they left. With the little money his father was able to bring out of Iran, Neusha opened a bookstore on Wilshire. Mostly poetry. Novels and magazines as well. All of it in Farsi. A few of us had been there and could say only the kindest things.

It is like being in high school again. When you were excited to do your homework. He even has the illustrated Rumi and the old stories of Farrokhzad. Such a lover of poetry, reminds me of an uncle of mine. The bookseller will recite Shamlu for you. Hafiz. He even knows some Googoosh songs by heart. Nice young man, inspired, romantic, a bit sad.

It was not uncommon to go to his bookstore to browse, exchange a few words and leave convinced, through your soul, that the world had gone off course and that to be Iranian was not to love the Shah or hate the Shah or support Khomeini or run from the new regime. To be Iranian was to be a poet. To be a lover of the words and worlds that our ancient relatives crafted so that we could better see our selves, both in and out of time.

To be a lover of Iran, to be of Iran is to be a lover of poetry, to be a poet! Nothing more! Nothing less!

Neusha insisted as we stood in his store nodding our heads, wondering how we had forgot such a simple truth.

In those times this was not an easy lesson to remember: 1978. 1979. 1980. 1981. 1982. 1983. A fallen king. A risen mystic. A hostage crisis that will play in history like games between stubborn children. A war with a neighbor over nothing. Forty-five thousand men dead for no gain of land or honor or pride. Two thirds of them younger than thirty years. We forgot the poetry. We fled. We forgot ourselves and from time to time claimed the king was false! The mystic is a fraud! Bring back the king and his son! Death to the king and his son! Stop this senseless war! Give us back our country! But with time we would forget even these ardent claims. Neusha was right; in the silence that followed those years, we remembered and returned to the poetry again and again, our first place of belonging, our first nation.

We did what we could to make a life of this life. The news from the television, from home, from our dreams, spun around us in a sticky web, and we kept our eyes focused on our work, our families, the new language. We did our best. Neusha had done his best and he was finished. He left a long letter. In it he explained the reasons for his actions: By setting fire to myself I am not only protesting the presence of the Iranian butcher Khomeini and his forthcoming trip to the United Nations, but also the poisonous activities of the pro-Shah elements and the ultraright policies of the Reagan administration . . . The next day Neusha stood in front of the Los Angeles Federal Building with a crowd protesting Khomeini's arrival. Without warning he poured two tins of motor oil over his head and clothes and did not, according to witnesses, pause before he lit a match. The fire burned for four minutes before bystanders wrestled the burning man down and hit out the flames. By that time 80 percent of his skin had blackened. His hair was gone. He could no longer see. He was thirty-one years old.

The police asked, Who does this to themselves?

The newspapers asked, Where in the world do people burn themselves alive?

The Americans around us asked, Why would anyone do such a thing?

We knew, but did not answer. We did not even discuss it because it was obvious, evident in each and every one of our selves. The published photos showed a man on fire. Fully upright, flames at all angles of his body. A scream frozen on his face. We knew the terror of the flame; we had craved it for months now, and his scream froze in our own throats, just above numb hearts. His burning flesh answered our desire to feel, to melt to belong belong belong.

And just like that, our dead joined us. And just like that, we belonged.

And those of us who paid attention to the silent events of nature looked at the yearly movements in our gardens and in the sky and thought to ourselves, We are not so different from them, but thanks be to God we are the only animals to suffer the migration of the soul, that labyrinthine route of the spirit that takes us not there and back but round and round and round.

CAVES

A WEEK AFTER the picnic and Saladin's sunken mood will not lift. The rug seller finds him asleep behind the warehouse and makes a casual suggestion.

Maybe you should take a few days off. To the ocean perhaps? I hear the girls wear next to nothing, and there is a sport with the waves. Go. Vacation is very important here. Go. Find some American energy.

One Thursday afternoon Saladin makes his way to the beach. Since he left, he has not been back and does not remember exactly how to get there. After half a day of walking and wrong buses he finds Santa Monica and, soon after, the sand. He takes his shoes off and moves north, his one untried direction. For a time the beach is spotted with all of the same people and diversions, one after another with their towels, umbrellas, sleep and suntan oil, again and again, like stamps on the sand. Then, after a time, nothing.

The emptiness is broken by the outlines of three large-bodied beasts that linger and stroll against the flat line of the sea. Saladin walks toward them to see if they are elephants, and if the elephants are as they were in the cinema, enormous gray-skinned puppets used to signify jungles or the circuses or human smallness. When he reaches them, he sees they are creatures unto themselves, with slow eyes and soft gazes and little care for the sadness of man. Around the elephants men and women in loose robes and sandals hit tambourines and sing. At the sight of Saladin they smile through their songs. Without listening too closely he can tell the words are not in English, but Hindi, the language of movies he would only go to if nothing from Hollywood was showing. He looks into their faces and they are not dark or round-mouthed or otherwise similar to the faces of Bombay actors and actresses; their features and colors are American, their joy and smiles American as well. Saladin moves past them, closer to the elephants, which amble in the shallow waters, ankles tied together by a long, loose rope, and watches as they suck up the sea in their trunks. Each time they spray themselves, Saladin shivers with delight.

Though he now knows enough English to approach, he has no desire to be a stranger at their strange party and takes one last look at the animals at play in the surf and then continues on his way. Behind him the voices of men and women rise and fall, and Saladin turns back to see them dancing and singing, their happy smiles directed at no one.

Farther north the land begins to vary. What was flat sand and flat sea is broken now by great volcanic outcroppings that rise up like pyramids. In the sea the rocks take and take the slap of waves, and Saladin stares for long enough to realize this contact never stops. All day and all night and all year and perhaps since the beginning, the rocks have taken the waves, and he turns around to find the land behind him soft and shifting, and he thinks even this edge, this end of America, will soon be eaten by the great sea. For calm he looks at the sky and follows a formation of pelicans as they soar in a low, easy glide, their eyes and beaks and bony wings made of a certain strength and survival from long long ago.

By late afternoon he is north of Malibu and the beach has given way to high sandstone bluffs, craggy and pocked with hundreds of small, deep caves. He moves from one to another until he finds an entrance that rises above the height of his head and stretches past the width of his shoulders, a passageway into which he can fit. Only then does he walk in, and only then does the cave make dark a day that was bright, and loud an ocean that outside was hushed and quiet. In the first darkness he cannot see and must stand still and listen to the sounds of the sea, which are huge and elaborately detailed now, in some constant flux between crash and hush. After all his time on the beach, the three nights and those early days, he has never heard these sounds—the pop of bubbles and roll of thousands of tiny stones—of the sea. He bends to feel if the cave floor is damp, and when his eyes finally make out its shape and distance, there is only sand and a pile of charred wood inside a circle of stones. He cannot see the end of it and pushes farther in, upright and then crouched and then on hands and knees. He comes to a sandy back wall and stops, sits up against it, and in an instant he is both tired and glad, relieved to have found this dark, hidden hole.

It is not his first cave.

In the first cave there were men—fathers, uncles, cousins and brothers—to fill the high stone cavern with song and smoke for the ceremony that would clear Saladin of his foreskin and so place on his name and face and shoulders the mantle of man. To himself he was still a boy, and when the knife came and then the blood and the pain, he cursed his father and sought out Ali's eyes and found them, sought his brother's hand and found it, craved his brother's voice and heard it, steady and proud.

Tomorrow it will be better, Saladin jaan. Tomorrow they will all love you more. Aufareen Saladin.

In this second cave there is no such love. The sand and stones of this vacant hole promise him nothing of a tomorrow where there is more. Saladin waits for the hollow feeling to pass and closes his eyes only to find, behind their lids, a dozen fat and menacing shapes—short men with enormous cocks and hooked noses and nails, boys with the hands of giants, a donkey with no head—all twirling and pulsing in a grotesque display. Fright pushes his heart quickly against his chest and pops open his eyes, and he does not recognize where he is. How has he come to this haunted cave? How far has he gone from that first cave? His brother's soft hand? That pledged love?

Saladin grabs fitfully at the sand beneath his palms and tries to think clearly. He is Saladin Khourdi. He lives in America today. He worked for a rug seller yesterday, and he will work for the rug seller again tomorrow. He washes and eats at least once each day. Today he sits in a cave, on a vacation, resting. Once, not yesterday, but before, he was a boy surrounded and sworn to men who, by the fact of Saladin's many steps, no longer exist.

How?

How many steps from that first cave to this?

There were the steps he took with Ali, the two of them marching out of their maman's womb, one after another, and then the same steps of their boyhood where no one bothered to tell them apart, and their steps into that first cave and then to school, through youth and then in circles during the years of wondering and the terrible death, and finally the fast steps they ran straight out of the wet spring valley where they escaped not as Saladin or Ali, but as Khourdis, as brothers, as one.

Ali, where are you now?

Saladin asks of the nothing around him, and the nothing responds with itself. He does not know where Ali is, so his mind goes to the last time and thoughts of the night raid and the cold airplane hull, and all of it dries the saliva in his throat and Saladin tries to swallow, again and again, but there is no wetness, no flavor or stick, and for a few seconds he must work to keep calm, to think his throat loose and bring out water from a mouth so parched it is as if he has just eaten the handfuls of sand he plays with. He tries to get out from the cave, to go back to the beach, where there is more air, more wind, water and space to swallow or to shout, and as he begins to crawl, a memory locked in the body unlocks. Saladin freezes and lets his body, heart and head grow cold, grow brittle with the shock of remembering the first moment he walked away from his brother and the first moment his brother walked away from him.

Friday. A day of no school and sweets after lunch and chores in the pigeon coop.

The brothers woke early to sweep shit and feathers, water and feed the pigeons and wait patiently for their father to arrive. He would show just as the sun was in the center of the sky, and even though his suit smelled of opium and sleep still creased into his face, he made a great ritual of seriousness as he inspected each bird, checked their water tins and the quantity of seed left in the sack. The brothers knew the worth of their work by his pauses and nods, and if all was done to satisfaction, their father would make a show of inspecting them as well. He spoke gravely to tease them all the more.

Saladin jaan, it seems your wings are a bit dusty today.

A strong hand would tickle him gently in the ribs.

You are a mess. We cannot possibly send you out and away.

A joke between father and son, and week after week Saladin waited for it, for the hand and the laugh that came after, and even for the small terror that shook him at the thought of *out* or *away*. Out from what? Away to where? He would hold tight to his father's hand as the old man walked slowly from bird to bird to select the day's messenger.

Saladin and Ali could barely tell them apart. There were the well ones and the lame ones, and all the others looked the same. They watched their father carefully—his eyes and fingers and nose—as he touched and smelled and saw each bird separately, and there was always a neck more iridescent or eyes more alive or wings stronger against his tests, and that bird was chosen and carried out to the clearing, where their father took a single small note from his pocket and read it with great authority.

Agha Homayun. What is your wife cooking for dinner? Ghorbonet, Captain Khourdi.

He then rolled the paper around the ankle of the bird and fastened it with twine. When a bird was released, it always did the same thing: flew up first and then out and then away from the trio of Khourdi men, and the young brothers always cheered, for what, they could never say.

They spent the afternoon in wait.

And Saladin did not hesitate to ask.

But how, Baba? How does the pigeon know where our house is? How do they remember?

Instinct.

What is that?

It is the knowing of where you belong. And when.

The pigeons always returned at dusk, and the brothers had to hold still so as not to punch or bite or wrestle the other back from racing to grab the oblivious bird. Finally one was chosen to catch the bird, and the other was chosen to unwrap the note tied to its ankle. Their father would squint and read the news aloud.

Dearest Captain Khourdi, My wife is making lentil-and-lamb stew. Yours, Agha Homayun.

And then grunt.

Does that woman ever make anything else?

And the brothers would laugh, as if on cue from last week and the week before that, happy their father was happy, glad the bird had come back.

One Friday their mother forbade the coop. Saladin was six and Ali was almost eight. She refused to hear their protests of *But Baba wants* and *Baba will be mad if* and forced them into a cold bath for a coarse wash. She ordered them into their best wool short pants and took them to town, one in each hand, Saladin crying like a much younger child and his brother taking on the complicated mix of silence and anger that would mark him later, for the rest of his walking days.

They went to a new building that smelled of paint and sawdust and sweat. This first wait was like all first waits, long and without comfort, and the brothers grew stiff and impatient with their mother, the wasted afternoon and the half-dark room without games or birds. When true blackness fell and the screen grew bright and the voice of an invisible man filled the room, their boredom was gone and the brothers sat frozen in a wonder as painful as it was staggering.

Here one brother does and the other does not.

At six years old Saladin let go of all time. He forgot that he was a boy, that he belonged to a mother and a father and a brother and two, almost three, sisters and forwent all geography and alliances and let himself dissolve into the screen, become a self just a bit different from the self before, a bit less six, a bit less boy and a bit more shaped into the mold of the cinema seat, L-shaped and upright and stuck. Here he was first seduced by the carved lips of giantesses, the square jaws of suited men, the cars and enormous flying machines and jewels and guns of that other world that came at him without relent. He did not have a moment to turn to his mother or brother and ask, What? Where? How?

There was a story in that first film. Men and women needed to escape but were stuck in a town on the edge of the desert and the sea. There was a battle somewhere, yet there were comforting suggestions between the eyes of one of the men and one of the women throughout. The suggestions went from curiosity, to disgust, to some sort of pull Saladin had never seen, to relief and then to a sadness he had watched cloud his maman's eyes. There was a black-skinned man who sat at a black box and made music with his fingers. People sat around the black man and his black music box and drank and talked and cried and listened and waited to fly off in enormous metallic machines. All around and through Saladin marvel pulsed as everyone in the mountain town's first cinema asked themselves and each other, Where? Where? Where? For the first time in their lives the sight of their eyes did not stop at their peripheral vision but extended beyond 180 degrees to wrap all the way back around to the insides of their heads, and then down into their hearts, where they could see, in their imaginations, another world different from their world and the world of their mothers and fathers and all that came before. In the world on the screen they did not see themselves at all and wondered, If I do not exist in this world of shadow and light on the screen, then is that world real? And if it is real, then how can I enter it? And if I enter it, who will I be?

Ali! Ali! Ali, can you believe it?

His brother made no noise and Saladin turned his head from the screen to find him in a tight feigned sleep with eyes pressed closed and furrowed brows.

On the walk home his brother ran ahead, unfazed and shouting.

Hurry! Baba will have already sent the bird! We should be home before it gets back!

But Saladin and his mother did not hear him. They walked mute from enthrallment, and Saladin held his mother's hand and opened his eyes wider and wider on the old town and country around them, disappointed in all he saw. He asked his mother again and again.

Where was that?

Amreeka.

Yes, but where is it?

I will show you, jaan. One day we might see it together.

When they arrived, his father was on the porch, Ali already at his side.

If it is not back by now, it will not return.

His father kept a cigarette drooped in his lips and he whittled a small piece of wood with his knife.

It is near dark and the skies have clouded since the morning. These birds do not navigate under cloudy skies. They do not navigate well.

He announced it to everyone without looking up, and Saladin watched his mother as she walked past him into the house. His father shouted after her.

You think you can leave us to starve like this? Where is the dinner?

The first step away. Ali kept to the house, to their father, the mountains and the every-week sortie of pigeons.

It is beautiful how they return.

Saladin heard Ali explain to their sisters.

Beautiful like you. Watch. Today we will send them out, and this evening they come back, a life of circles . . .

And Saladin took to the cinema as if it were a cave or his mother's belly or the belly of some hungry monster that needed to eat a little piece of him every day. With his mother's blessing and pocket change he went every afternoon for film after film and burned with questions he took to the teachers at school, to his brother and father: Where? How? Can I? How can I? Only to receive answers of silence; ridicule; heavy-handed smacks that no longer hurt after a while because by eleven years Saladin was, to his own mind, gone.

One afternoon Ali came to follow Saladin as he left the cinema. Ali walked beside and did not say one kind word but teased Saladin for the long walk home.

Baba says you want to be like Maman, that you love the movies like a girl.

Saladin did not pause or restrain himself before reaching out for his brother's skin and tearing at it with all the force of his fingers and nails until their mother ran to pull them apart. She gave Saladin extra change to go back to the cinema and disciplined Ali with a hard smack.

There were the steps to the cinema that afternoon and then the steps home. The steps away from his mother's body, later that year, and then away from sisters and father and brother too. There were the steps into his imagination and away from the mountains. Finally there were the steps he took with Ali into the mountains and the steps he refused to take out of the plane. Life, a series of steps taken, avoided, done right, done wrong.

In the near dark of the cave Saladin looks over his hands, one and then the other. He tries to bring back the feeling of his brother's flesh beneath them as it was when they fought that day. He aches to feel Ali here under his fingers, palms and nails, but nothing comes. His hands fall to the sand again and he picks up the cool particles and lets them run through his fists, handful by handful, until all of his thoughts dissolve and he is no more than tired, no more than hungry and cold.

Outside the cave the day has given up its brilliance. Saladin walks to the water's edge to see the sky speak out in dark oranges and light blues. At the far end of this horizon a group of osprey are at work. They float high above the water, still in a steady wind, their expert eyes cast down and focused on whatever moves just beneath the surface.

Saladin too has flown, has known the sky well enough to remember the flat way light shone up off the face of the sea, the strange way, aloft, his thoughts belonged more to the sky than spaces inside his own head. For a time, after the plane took off, the engines vibrated so loudly he could not think. The cold of the night had seeped into his bones and he stood after a few clumsy falls. He watched the pilots through the narrow door of the cockpit, and once he was certain they would stay as they had been, stuck before the enormous rectangular glass windows, smoking one cigarette after another, clueless of their stowaway, Saladin pulled himself up. He crawled to the back of the plane, where he found a pile of parachutes, some boxes strapped down to hooks and a small, egg-shaped window that allowed him his first view of the huge, sad ocean; the empty view of the earth from above as only the birds know. Like the rest of the men and women and children of the Iranian exodus, Saladin looked down and felt a great stagnation, the powerful tranquillity of having been forsaken by the earth, cast up, absolved of all ground-bound responsibilities. For this period of time he did not care to see another inch of land, did not care to arrive, to touch America's dreamed-of shore. In this moment there was only this great height and its proximity to the empires of angels and silences, and that was enough; peace unto itself; a home where he might, at last, rest.

Ahead the ospreys dip and rise with great purpose. Saladin watches as they dive down, quick and sure, and snatch small silver fish in their spread-out talons. He runs his hands over his face to make sure he is seeing it all as it is, life plucked up and out of the water, still alive, and flown up and over him into the green mountains of Malibu just behind. And, yes. It is. The method and determination of the birds is so precise and mesmerizing that Saladin does not notice that the water of the waves has reached his feet and sinks his shoes deeper into the wet sand.

Time and time again the birds curl their claws ever tighter about the guts and gills of the fish whose muscles spasm as they convulse in the dry air. Saladin makes a game of counting the twitching silver bodies that soar above him and shake the last flashes of a sea life from their skin. He sees that in every catch there is a moment when both bird and fish suspend, equal, between drowning and flight, and for one second it is unclear which is the fiercer of the two desires. A few catches fail and the birds clumsily drop the fish back into the big sea and fly, tired and finished, behind Saladin. They pass over him with their large white wings spread low to the ground, their bellies hungry and without, and Saladin cannot help but hunch his own shoulders and duck his head under their empty, open claws, a man crouched down for fear that the fate of the fish is his fate, that he is no more than a creature to be plucked off the earth, pulled up from the life he lives and taken far off, somewhere else, to die.

He jerks his feet out from the suck of wet sand and stands back from the water. After a time the birds are fed and gone and the western horizon is empty. Saladin stands at the edge of white wash and listens for the thin whispers of the leviathan. When nothing from beyond calls, he turns his bones south and walks on.

ACKNOWLEDGMENTS

The poem cited on page 235 is an excerpt from "The Peacock's Response" by Farid ud-Din Attar's beautiful book *The Conference of Birds.*

I am happily indebted to those institutions and individuals who supported me during the writing of this book. My sincere gratitude to the Whiting Foundation, Emory University's Fiction Fellowship and to Mara Batlin and David Deniger for the generous use of their serene retreat in the Santa Lucia foothills. I am grateful for the detailed and intelligent research assistance of Jane Wongso Suhardjo. A great swell of appreciation for the steadfast (and patient) professional guidance of Anton Mueller, Alexandra Pringle and Ellen Levine, without whom publishing a book would be an insurmountable dream.

As always my heart goes (and goes and goes) to Ariel Ross, Keenan Norris, John Myer, Saneta deVouno Powell, Isabel Wilkerson, Micheline Marcom and, most especially, Timothy Kelly and Kamran and Fereshteh Khadivi, for their ready encouragement and distraction, inspiration, and light.

A NOTE ON THE AUTHOR

Laleh Khadivi was born in Esfahan, Iran, in 1977. In the aftermath of the Islamic Revolution her family fled, finally settling in Canada and then the United States. Khadivi received her MFA from Mills College and was a Creative Writing Fellow in Fiction at Emory University. In 2008 she received The Whiting Writers' Award. In 2009 she published her first novel, *The Age of Orphans*. Laleh Khadivi lives in California.

A NOTE ON THE TYPE

The text of this book is set in Bembo. This type was first used in 1495 by the Venetian printer Aldus Manutius for Cardinal Bembo's *De Aetna*, and was cut for Manutius by Francesco Griffo. It was one of the types used by Claude Garamond (1480–1561) as a model for his Romain de L'Université, and so it was the forerunner of what became standard European type for the following two centuries. Its modern form follows the original types and was designed for Monotype in 1929.